REBIRTH

The second book in The Judas Syndrome series

Michael E. Poeltl

Michael E. Poeltl

This book is a work of fiction. The characters, incidents, and dialogue are drawn from the author's imagination and are not to be construed as real. Any resemblance to actual events or persons, living or dead, is entirely coincidental.

FIRST EDITION

ISBN 978-0-9813168-1-9

To the past

May you be remembered.

Michael E. Poeltl

Power can be taken, but not given. The process of the taking is empowerment in itself.
Gloria Steinem - Journalist

Michael E. Poeltl

Sara Speaks....

I can't find my son. Anxiety overwhelms me. My heart pounds as I rush through the compound, in my panic it seems more like a maze than the place I'd called home the past eight years. *Where is my son?* The night comes alive as search lights expose the darkness between buildings, igniting the tight spaces a boy of eight might find himself. A sinister thought enters my head: *My mortal enemy currently shares this space with u*s. A renewed sense of urgency overcomes me, my pace quickens.

*****

Your Father would have so loved you. You were a blessing when you were born; you were a mystery when you were conceived and a terrible struggle while I carried you seven months in my belly. Seven months: it's not really long enough, but you seemed to time your arrival eerily close to the date of another's departure.

This place is like a concentration camp you'd see on TV, when there was TV. Something from a Second World War movie. Did we live through the Third World War? Hard to say. Color is absent here: the walls are a battleship grey, the floors a polished concrete. Not ideal surroundings for a baby to grow up in, but at least you grew up.

When we arrived you were very small and still at my breast.

Somehow we had escaped a plague that ravaged much of the surviving world.

Children are very important; so many died from this plague that took the very young and very old. Most adults over sixty years old and those under the age of twelve died soon after the Apocalypse, choked to death by fall-out, while those who survived were left to suffer this final indignity some months later. A plague, a flu of some design. I have worked closely with the doctors here, and they have not been able to succinctly label the disease that had methodically killed off so many.

The base was designed to train special ops and special forces in the war against terror. It has only a skeleton crew assigned to it, though it was expecting an influx of 1000 soldiers and their families the month following the end of life as we knew it. The base is well protected, with steel walls reaching heights of 20 feet in places, outfitted with watch towers, a stockade, family housing, a mess hall, hospital and the central training and parade grounds. It even has a greenhouse.

The parade grounds are framed with civilian vehicles, RV's, camper vans, cars and trucks of all shapes and sizes. They belong to those who fled the devastation to the south and came north. I recall the many motorcades we witnessed traveling north, right past Joel's house, where we had hidden out. We were fourteen friends, caught in something as unfathomable as the end of the world. Teenagers, whose families had all been wiped out by one violent act against humanity. I remember talking to people as they stopped at the house. They said they were going on a *feeling*, going north.

The Sergeant told me that barely a year after the majority of civilians had arrived, the plague had hit the base, and hundreds were quarantined. Almost all of them died, eventually. The base lost many of their own to the mysterious plague as well. The army doctors worked day and night to suppress the disease, to stop it in its tracks. In doing so, the hospital lost over 75% of its staff.

Finally the plague had run its course. No more were dying, no more were feeling feverish or showing red spots on their necks and torsos. Those who had survived, roughly half including both the base personnel and civilians, would carry on, burn their dead and start again.

*****

I remember asking about the water planes my friends and I had seen putting out forest fires as we drove back to town, returning from our camping trip the day after the Reaper had followed through on his promise.

"They flew out of Kingston Air force base," explained the captain. She removed her hat as she spoke. Her short blonde hair fell around her high cheek bones. She was an attractive woman, but she'd suffered an unimaginable loss, and the lines in her face mapped that story. "It's two days' drive west of us. They were retrofitted to do that job, those planes. They would load up on water at Elle Lake, and run water dumps all over the area. Now, you said you were a good two hour drive south of here, Sara?"

"Yes, about that." I replied.

"I'd say the planes would have penetrated just south of that, and then west." She confirmed.

"We saw three or four at a time."

"Yes, you would have. They employed thirty odd. They ran day and night for about 48 hours following the attack, and then, nothing."

"Nothing?" My voice cracked.

"We lost contact with them." The captain's tone was thoughtful.

"What happened to them?" I asked.

"Fatigue. The pilots wanted to keep flying. Keep up the momentum. Best we could tell, two of the bigger planes slammed into each other and then into the control tower while attempting to land and fuel up. They wiped out everyone, and with them any chance for the other pilots to continue their work."

"That's so awful."

"We sent a patrol to investigate, and this was their conclusion." Her eyes met mine.

"No wonder you never came for us." My friends and I had held onto hope of a rescue for weeks after the sighting, believing that they had seen us, and that they would come for us. But they never did.

"Even if we were made aware of your existence, it's unlikely we would have come for you. We were undermanned ourselves and had been ordered to stay put."

"Makes sense I guess." But I wondered what my life would have been like had they come for us. Would Joel still be with me? Perhaps we would have succumbed like the others to the plague, like the captain's husband and daughters had.

*****

The world wasn't always like this, and perhaps one day it will be better. The military houses us now. They have graciously put us up here in the hope that you will survive, have children of your own and rebuild. That may sound like a lot to put on a child not yet eight years old, but know that you are very special, and not just in the way only a mother can know.

You would have had it so good in *life*. That's what we called it *before* the Reaper dropped the bombs: *life*. We were all someone else, kids barely out of high school. The *Grimm Reaper* as the media had coined him, was a mad man. A man, an organization, a country, no one really knew. The threat seemed almost laughable. But he wasn't laughing. He had demands that were never met, he had crazy ideals that required religions and governments to disappear. The things he asked were impossibilities. So he showed us just how serious he was. The initial blasts killed our families. My friends and I had been spared, having taken a camping trip that weekend, *the weekend.* And when we returned, our worlds were changed forever. We, fourteen of us at first and within seven months only eight, managed to stay alive, at my boyfriend's house in the country. We felt privileged, chosen to survive, to rebuild.

More than nine years ago my life was very different. Was I lucky to have experienced life in all its normalcy, in all its abundance? I think so, I still have my memories. Though sometimes my memories seem like little more than movies, something from someone's imagination.

The people here, the soldiers, they believe that much of the planet has fared better than our little corner. To believe is a powerful thing. It can keep you from despair, it can offer you salvation. *Belief* is sometimes all you have, your faith. I lost it once…

Part One
Chapter One

You think you know someone. Really know them. You think they're in control of their thoughts, themselves. You give them the benefit of the doubt, believe that they will make the right choices that they'll make you proud. Do they sense that? And when you're trusting someone to lead you in the right direction... are those who lead more susceptible to the expectations of those who would follow? We're not all cut out to lead. Some don't choose to lead. It is thrust upon them and when the burden proves too much to bear, they wish it away like a dead limb, weighing heavier each day the wish is not granted.

I've often asked myself, in Joel's defense, how might I have performed under the same circumstances? Would I cloak myself in a drug induced haze, would I become paranoid with power? Would I finally kill myself, knowing so many would suffer for my actions?

Is it any different than what the Reaper had done? To paraphrase Joel's note, scribbled on stationary from his mother's hardware store, found in his room, *our* room, on his childhood desk; *"I know now that a single action can put in motion a series of repercussions. Should that action be positive, the repercussions are rewarding, but when that action is negative, so too are the events to follow. A single action can change you forever. Sometimes, if the deed is large enough, if the intent evil enough, the results can be disastrous."*

I heard it in my head as though he were speaking to me, whispering in my ear, and I wept. What irony is this? What sadness this implies, such a good man, tormented and turned. Could this happen to me? Time will tell. I will tell. And only then will I know.

*****

The rains had returned. Connor was dead. Joel was holed up in his bedroom, and those of us remaining felt more victimized now than when the Reaper had unleashed his evil upon the world. The rain, a blessing to us, to the whole world, would take a backseat to our internal demons. Incapable of rejoicing in this miracle, we waited on Joel to emerge from his self-induced confinement.

"He's in there," I whispered to Earl as I paced just outside Joel's bedroom door. "He's quiet though. I'm really worried, Earl." I picked at the skin peeling from my fingertips, the nails having been chewed to the quick long ago.

"Sara, let him be. Jesus, we're barely an hour into Connor's funeral. Imagine what's going on in his head." Earl could have been right; maybe he was just decompressing. But the look on his face, after what Gareth had done, after Connor had been shot… it was almost as devastating a sight as the execution itself.

I decided to knock on the door, lightly, so that he knew I was there. Earl shook his head in disapproval, but remained silent.

"Go away!" Joel shouted. I jumped. Such pain in his voice, such … regret. Earl threw his hands up and backed away from the door. "I'd let him be for a while, Sara. He's obviously got to work through this on his own."

"No one should have to work through this on their own, Earl. I'm worried about him." My eyes flew back to the door as we heard first a thumping sound coming from within, then a murmur and another shout. "Not yet!" Joel repeated. My skin crawled and goose bumps overtook me.

Earl gently placed a hand on my shoulder and rubbed. I felt more anxious at his touch than comforted. I removed his hand and wiped away a tear. He smiled narrowly at me. I'd never been able to read Earl. He was never my type: intelligent yes, but his intensity had always frightened me. His mind was like a runaway train.

"I have to get back to Sonny; just thought I'd see what's what up here." He turned to leave, but I stopped him.

"Earl, you're not planning anything are you?" The idea that we might now go to war with the flags was not something I could stomach. Not so soon after losing Connor. Couldn't we just bury our dead and mourn for a time? Earl shrugged and smirked as though there were little else to do. "Earl…." I trailed off as he went down the hall and into Skylab.

The flags (so-called because of the ominous flag they carried, declaring themselves an autonomous nation of survivors) had been a cruel interruption into an otherwise solid foundation built on the ashes of the past. We had survived a nuclear holocaust. We had built a life for ourselves, and then the flags showed up. Led by Gareth, a man possessed by the idea of weeding secret Reaper sympathizers from surviving groups like our own and executing them to further his twisted purpose, the flags posed a threat unlike anything we'd imagined. His group consisted of nearly sixty upon his arrival at our door, but after a third party attacked our house from the devastated woods, he was left with little more than twenty. We retook control of our home and our lives by ousting the flags, ordering them away, and relieving them of their weapons and morale, or so we thought.

But they had returned, executing Connor in front of us after they'd caught us unaware. A sympathizer, they called him - Connor, before they shot him in the head. A sympathizer to the Reaper's ideals, as if anyone would claim such madness after the hell the *Grimm Reaper* had unleashed on us all.

 Left alone to contemplate further what scheme Earl and Sonny were planning, my eyes fell again to Joel's bedroom door. I pushed my hands against the frame and slowly lowered my head until my forehead gently rested against the door. My cheek made contact with the cool wood. Eyes closed, I listened for movement, a sound, something that would let me in. What horrors was he experiencing in there? "Let me in," I whispered to the door.

A moment later, Caroline came up the stairs and took my hand. I resisted, hesitant to leave my vigil at the door. Her eyes were red and swollen. The sight of her made me break down. Caroline followed in turn. I pulled her close, and we hugged. And we cried.

*****

Caroline finally released herself from our embrace and rubbed her eyes hard. "What, what do you think he's doing in there Sara?" she asked.

"I wish I knew. I wish he'd let me in." My arms crossed defensively as I looked back at the door.

"Is Joel going to be alright, you think?"

"I don't know, Caroline." I couldn't hide my own inability to read him anymore. God, we had grown so far apart in such a short time. It felt like a microsecond. From *I love you* to a break up, separate rooms and a blow out that sent him off to who knows where, in search of who knows what! "I don't have those answers."

"Should we get back to the others?"

Reluctantly, I agreed. Sucking in a deep breath, I pushed my fingers through her long, somewhat greasy blonde hair, as though tidying her up for an interview. When I reached the ends I carefully patted them down on her shoulders. "Okay, let's go see what they're doing." Holding hands, we walked down the hall and into the addition, where the rest of the house now gathered.

We walked into a fierce speech, told in unwavering absolutes. Phrases like *'we must'*, and *'how could we'* and *'how dare they'*. It was an impressive rant, not unlike many of the one-sided conversations he'd mastered in the past. No one could put together an argument like Earl, and in this, he was making his stand.

"This is not how this is going to end!" He pushed on, while a captive audience of our peers stood in silence. "This isn't an *ending*. This is a new *beginning*. Gareth and his flags cannot be allowed to just walk off into the sunset."

"What are you proposing, Earl?" I blurted out, angry he'd gone and done exactly what I had feared. The room held a distinct sense of immediacy. It permeated the air and made it hard to breathe.

"I propose we *fight*, Sara!" He glared at me, the devil in his eyes.

"Why would you want to pull us all back into this now, after having lost so much!" I studied the group, panning the room while their eyes betrayed them. A perfect moment to rally the troops perhaps - to offer them a solution. On the other hand, an excellent opportunity for someone to take control, to give the group a reason, purpose. Did Earl know what he was doing? Did he see what he was becoming?

"Whoa, Earl," Caroline broke in. She was shaken and it resonated in her voice. "What are we talking about here? Running after the flags? Hunting them down? Two wrongs don't make a right." She was pleading to the group now. "Right? I don't want to fight anymore. How could any of you want to *fight* anymore?"

"What else is there to do?" Sonny phrased it as more of a statement than a question.

"Rebuild," I said. "Rebuild, regroup. Jesus, anything but get into another fight!"

"What if they come back?" added Kevin. I wasn't surprised. I didn't much like Kevin. His allegiance would fall to anyone that took the initiative to lead. He was weak.

"Listen to me, Joel is still here, *okay*? He's still our leader, by vote! It's his call whether we send people to track down the flags, not yours." I pointed at Earl.

"I'm allowed to have an opinion aren't I, Sara? It may not be the same country anymore, but as far as we're concerned, it's still free." He glared at me.

I readdressed the group. "All I'm saying is not to get caught up in Earl's hype. We don't need to throw away our lives. Connor wouldn't want to be *avenged*."

"Says you!" Earl may have respected Joel's leadership, but he would not concede the point. "Connor was a good man and a good soldier. And he went to the grave for all of us! All he needed to do was say the word and we'd have all died that day in defiance. But he knew that, and he died *for* us!" He sat down on a stool by the west windows, exhausted. "And it's eating me up inside…" His words were not falling on deaf ears. Freddy, Sonny and Kevin approached Earl and stood next to him.

Seth and Sidney did not move, positioned at the east wall, guns dangling from their uncertain grips. I approached Seth and knelt beside him. We exchanged looks. He was no more ready to go to war with the flags than I was. I recognized indecision in Sidney's face. Admittedly, a small part of me cherished the idea of going to war with the flags. I was still reeling from the events that lead to Connor's death.

I turned to watch as Kevin stood and stared out the west windows. The forest still resembled something from a children's Halloween picture book. Stripped bare of their leaves, the trees stood as dark silhouettes against a grey-black background. It had been raining on and off since Joel had returned from the woods, after having left us at Connor's graveside.

It was approaching 8:30 pm when I heard a door shut. Joel was moving. I rushed out of Skylab and across the hall. His bedroom door was open and the bathroom door now closed. I pressed my ear up against the door and listened. In my peripheral vision I could see the group gathered by the addition entrance.

There was a murmuring inside the bathroom, followed by a hard thump. Something broke. I jumped back. Looking for encouragement from the others, I slowly approached the bathroom door again. They were frozen in place, unable or perhaps unwilling to move.

I pressed my ear to the door and heard Joel inside rustling around. I knocked lightly and tried to speak but nothing made it past the lump in my throat. He was ignoring me. How long would this continue? How long could I let it continue? Seth was behind me, gently pulling me away from the door. I held up a restraining hand.

"I'll be all right," I smiled, although I felt like I was in a dream at that moment. My head swam with emotions and memories, making me dizzy. "I need to be alone right now." Seth nodded and released his delicate grip. I walked into Joel's bedroom and sat on the bed. A low rumble of thunder rolled through the clouds overhead.

I wanted to pray, but felt there was no longer anyone listening. My faith had been shaken by the return of the flags, and the devastation they left in their wake. I couldn't bring myself to pray at Connor's funeral. Should I have felt I'd let him down by foregoing a prayer? Will his soul not rest now? Crossing my heart I bowed my head in prayer. "Amen," I muttered aloud after completing my appeal.

As I panned the room, I felt alienated and lonely. The foreign feeling I got from this place, where I first told Joel I loved him, where we shared so much of ourselves, hurt me deeply.

I stood and walked towards his desk, where three pages of stationary rested. The top page had been filled top to bottom with Joel's handwriting. He'd never had a very attractive script. But this scrawl was especially hectic. This writing was done in haste, by a hand that wanted to write as much as possible as fast as possible and move on.

I sat down to read.

Chapter Two

*B*lank Page, Blank Mind, Blank Brain, Blank man. *Blink and Blank man disappears, blink and Blank man disappears. Blink, and nobody cares. Blink blinky, blink blinky, blink Bitch! If I could, I'd blink, if only I could blink. I'd be Blinky, blinking. Blank man would disappear.*

I frowned as I struggled to understand. Was *he* Blank man? No, he wished he were Blank man. Or was it Blinky he wished he was? Was Blank man the angel? He wanted Blank man to disappear. He wanted to erase something, a memory, an action… a person.

I read on.

"I know now that a single action can put in motion a series of repercussions. Should that action be positive, the repercussions are rewarding, but when that action is negative, so too are the events to follow. A single action can change you forever. Sometimes, if the deed is large enough, if the intent evil enough, the results can be disastrous."

This verse was well thought out and easily understood, but I was still confused. What *action* was he referring to? Was this written to express his view on what the Reaper had unleashed on humanity, or was this something more personal?

"What did you do, Joel?" I whispered, my hands covering my mouth as tears flowed down my cheeks. I looked back at the poem. Was Blank man Connor? Could he really have thought Connor and I had been…? Of course he could. He was capable of believing anything. He had confronted Connor on the subject before hitting him. The memory of that moment would never leave me. "Please, no. Please tell me you didn't, Joel." But the more I thought it through, the more likely it was that he had somehow orchestrated the execution of his best friend, and if he did, how could I ever love him again?

I read and reread the poem. I broke it down line by line on the stationary while writing my insights down on another sheet of paper.

Blank Page, Blank Mind, Blank Brain, Blank man. What was he trying to say here? He saw a blank page, nothing yet written, he had a blank mind again repeated in blank brain, suggesting he himself either couldn't remember something or didn't want to remember. Finally he mentioned Blank man. This character could be one of three people I decided. The angel, Connor, or himself. I read on.

Blink and Blank man disappears, blink and Blank man disappears. With an action he was able to block out the Blank man, making him disappear. Should this have been taken literally? If so, perhaps the Blank man was Connor. But it also might better describe Joel separating himself from something.

Blink, and nobody cares. Blink blinky, blink blinky, blink Bitch! No one cares… He felt no one would care if Blank man went away, no one would notice, or that the Blank man is worthless. He became repetitive now. He was hell-bent on snuffing out the Blank man. He became frustrated. He couldn't do it. His inner turmoil was surfacing.

If I could, I'd blink, if only I could blink. I'd be Blinky, blinking. He knew he needed to do this thing, to erase the Blank man, but felt powerless to do so. He would go to extremes to make Blank man disappear.

Blank man would disappear. He needed Blank man to disappear.

I summarized everything I'd been writing down. The conclusion was more revealing, and upsetting than I could have imagined.

Blank man *was* Joel. He was deeply disturbed. He felt worthless. He'd done something that he couldn't forgive himself for. He needed to stop the Blank man. He needed to stop himself. The question was, could he? Could he change? No, nothing in this spoke of change. He wanted to disappear…

The writing started with *Blank page*, he wanted to start again.

I suddenly noticed how silent it was. Had water been running in the bathroom? I looked automatically at my watch. 10:30pm. I'd been toiling over the poem for nearly two hours. I placed my hands at my lower back and stretched, tilting my head back, rolling my neck.

"What is he doing in there?" I wondered aloud.

A muffled cry rang through the bathroom wall as Joel thrashed in the tub. Alarmed, I jumped up from the desk and ran into the hall. I pressed my ear against the bathroom door but all was again silent. "Joel," I said tentatively. "Joel?" I knocked again. Nothing.

Sidney rounded the corner out of the addition. I waved him over.

"Something's wrong, Sid. He's not answering. Something's wrong."

"Joel?" he yelled. I looked at him with my best pained expression.

"Please Sid, kick it in." I pleaded. Sidney nodded and kicked the bathroom door in.

Chapter Three

Nothing could have prepared us for the scene inside. I pushed past Sidney and stopped cold when I spotted the bright red water in the tub. I lived a thousand different scenarios in that moment. As the seconds passed the picture became more and more surreal.

"No." I muttered. "No, no, no, no, no, no, no, no." My head shook from side to side, my face tightened and my throat went dry. "NO!" I shouted. I screamed. "NO! JOEL! NO!" I fell hard on my knees to the tiled floor and thrust my arms into the cold water. Pulling Joel free of the icy wetness, I gasped as I saw the life drain from his face.

"Jesus Christ!" Sid cried from behind me. "What the fuck!" I looked up at him and suppressed my own urge to lose it. I needed to be smart here. I needed to save Joel.

"Sid," I said. He didn't respond. "SID!" I shouted. His eyes focused on mine.

"Yeah?"

"Help me move Joel to the floor."

He snapped into action and grabbed Joel's feet. We struggled to move the dead weight over the side and onto the floor. Blood trickled from his forearm, soaking the floor mat.

"Sid, take off your belt." He reacted without as much as a pause. "Now wrap it around his forearm, above the wound, and pull it as tight as you can." Oh God, the wound. What had he used, a skill saw? I checked his pulse. The heartbeat was barely there, but there was hope. Had he been submerged for long? I listened at his nose for breath. How much blood had he lost? How would we ever replace it? How was I going to close this wound? He'd cut things I was sure I couldn't mend. We would have to resort to amputation.

"Sara?" I could hear the panic in Sid's voice. "Sara, is he alive?"

"Yes." I could barely think now. I tried to remember the minuscule training I'd been given at the clinic and my stints at the hospital during my co-op.

"Will he be okay?" His eyebrows threaded together over his frightened stare.

That depended on the amount of time he had to bleed out, I thought. "Joel can't have been like this for long. I only just heard the bath water shut off." The makeshift tourniquet was doing its job: the blood had stopped flowing from Joel's forearm. Sid held his ground, hovering over Joel's pale body, applying pressure to the arm with his right knee while pulling up on the belt.

"So, what now, what do we do now?"

I was working on that. What next? Shit I'd never done this. I'd never even *seen* this done. Would he slip into a coma? It depended on the blood loss.

"Talk to him, Sid. Slap his face, try to wake him up." I got to my feet and realized just how weak I had become. I found support on the counter and collected myself. "Stay with him while I get my books."

When I charged out of the bathroom, I nearly ran into the others. They were speechless. Watching. I moved past them frantically on my way to the bedroom. I dug around the couch until I found my medical textbooks under a pile of papers.

"Can we help?" Seth hovered in the doorway. "Can I help?"

"Boil some water and find me some clean linens." Flipping through the pages, I came to a section on amputation. Scanning the technical illustrations and brief explanations, I gave him another order. "Find something metal, wide but thin, maybe 6 inches square. We'll need a saw, a couple of gloves, alcohol and fire as well." Just scanning the steps to a successful modern day amputation told me I had no chance. I would have to amputate like a field surgeon in the Civil War.

Seth ran out into the hall and communicated my orders to the others. I was scared to death. Maybe one of the boys - possibly Earl- could do the cutting while I supervised. "It needs to be able to cut through bone," I shouted out to them. "The saw." My hand rose to my mouth, shaking uncontrollably. "Be strong," I whispered to myself. "He needs you."

Back in the bathroom, Sid had worked some color back into Joel's face with all the slapping. "Nothing," he reported. "Nothing's happening, Sara. Shouldn't he have woken up by now?"

"It's just as well, Sid. We're taking the arm off below the elbow." A look of horror struck him. My chin began to tremble but I forced myself to stay coherent. "It's the only way we can save him. The damage is too severe. I don't have the tools or the training to fix that." I pointed at the ruined arm. The soft flesh I so prized, the flesh of the arm I would rest my head upon while we drifted off to sleep. The skin I would put my lips to and swear was softer. And now, I was going to remove it.

The group returned with the requested items, Seth leading the way. "Where would you like everything?" he asked.

"Let's just do it here, on the floor," I answered. They placed everything on the counter. I poured the boiling water on Joel's arm and open wound. If ever he would wake up, surely that would have caused it. The alcohol was next. Then I sterilized the saw: a small saw with a thin cutting surface.

"It's a bone saw," said Earl. "For hunting."

"That should work."

I positioned the saw and closed my eyes. One quick push should make it through the muscle, I thought. Then four or five hard pulls through the bone and then more muscle. Less than ten strokes should do it. I felt sick at the thought. Could I have ever been a surgeon? "Fuck it," I said, as I wiped my forehead with my forearm and mouthed a prayer.

Chapter Four

"Sid," I ordered, "hold his arm down at the bicep and don't let it shift around as I cut." Earl circled round me, took Joel's hand and pushed down hard. With Sid at my left and Earl at my right, I wiped the sweat from my eyes and pushed the blade into Joel's lean muscled forearm.

"Jesus," whispered someone above us.

I dared not stall for long. I continued the grisly work on Joel's arm and upon hitting the bone, slowed considerably. I struggled for a moment. The blade warped as I realized it was stuck in the bone. I pulled at it roughly, wishing desperately for the job to be done. A scraping sound made everyone wince.

Suddenly Joel's eyelids sprang back, and his eyes bulged out of their sockets. His back arched violently and a scream burst from his mouth. He looked down at his arm, the saw in my hand and his friends gathered around, their faces white as ghosts at this unexpected turn. He wailed once more. Then his eyes rolled to the back of his head and he slipped into a comatose state.

I was frozen in place, too shocked and sickened to move.

"Let me, Sara." Earl took the saw from me. His right hand still holding down Joel's, he used his left to free the blade and continue the cut. In four short tugs he had separated Joel's forearm from the rest of his body.

Earl looked to me for further instructions. "Uh, heat the plate," I remembered, feeling my composure return. The metal plate was set up on the sink and a fire lit beneath it. Joel's severed hand twitched on the floor and I moved away from it, pulling myself up to the counter. "When its red hot, use the gloves to carry it over to the open wound and press it against his arm." When Freddy complied I turned my head and shook.

"It's really smoking, Sara." The stench of burnt flesh had permeated the room. Sid and Earl were literally waving the smoke away from their faces as Freddy continued to push the plate to Joel's stump.

"Dump some of the alcohol on it and remove the metal." Skin pulled away along with the plate as Fred removed it, but it was working. "More alcohol and heat the plate again."

We repeated the process a few more times until the flesh and muscle and bone were charred at the stump. "Apply the antibiotic cream and wrap it in the linens." It was my final order of the day. I was exhausted, and nauseated. The heat of so many bodies in that small bathroom, and the smell sent me into the hall and then into Joel's bedroom, where I gave myself permission to go to pieces.

"Would you like us to place him on the bed, Sara?" asked Caroline, leaning in through the doorway.

I looked up from Joel's desk, tears streaming down my cheeks. Caroline knelt down beside me.

"Look at my hands, Caroline." I said, shaking. "We... *I* just took off Joel's *arm*." My hands were stained red, leaving gory marks on everything I touched.

Caroline gently pulled me up from the desk chair. "Let's get you cleaned up."

We walked down to the bathroom on the main floor, passing the scene as our friends cleaned up the mess on the second floor. I caught a glimpse of Earl through the haze of smoke and bodies, gripping Joel's disembodied hand in his. He was hitting Kevin with it, as though it were a prop. I hadn't the energy to confront him, but what an asshole! I stared them both up and down- Kevin and Earl. They must have felt the burn of my gaze as their eyes met mine. "Assholes," I mouthed. Earl quickly put the hand in a bag and sent Kevin to the yard with it.

I never understood Earl. I always felt as though he hadn't given himself the opportunity to vent, to *feel* after everything went to shit, after the Reaper. But upon witnessing that spectacle, playing with Joel's hand as though it were a toy, I think I understood him better. It wasn't that he hadn't allowed himself to feel. It was that he *couldn't* feel. He talked a good game, he made others feel, but he himself, I don't think he had the capacity. What did they call that in *life?* A psychopath?

*****

That evening no one slept. If they weren't in the addition, located over the 3 car garage (on guard duty), they were in the bedroom with Joel and I. I tended to him at his bedside. Earl remained in the addition, in Skylab, hopefully embarrassed over his actions in the bathroom. His thoughtlessness, his blatant disregard for my feelings and those of the others... to play with a severed limb, a limb that used to belong to your friend... It was beyond comprehension, and beyond contempt.

"Earl *is* an asshole," Caroline agreed after I'd told her what I'd seen.

"I wanted to jam it down his throat, see if he thought *that* was funny." I gazed at Joel as he slept under the covers. I held his right hand in mine and leaned in close to listen to his breathing. It was erratic. "He's going to become a real problem if Joel doesn't wake up..."

"Earl?"

"Yeah."

Our conversation ended with the arrival of Sonny. Sonny was one of Joel's biggest supporters, figuratively and literally. Sonny, though he had lost a fair bit of weight over the past few months (like the rest of us) still carried a substantial frame, big-boned and muscular.

"Hey, Sara, Caroline."

"Hey, Sonny," I answered. Caroline smiled and nodded.

"Can I talk to you, Sara?" He eyed Caroline. "Outside?"

I looked at Caroline and passed Joel's hand to her. "Can you stay with him awhile?"

"No problem." Caroline took my place at the bedside. I followed Sonny down the staircase and out the front door.

"How are you holding up?" I asked him, hands in my pockets. The night sky was clouding over; a breeze hit us from the south, warm for January.

Sonny took a seat on the concrete porch. I stepped around the dark discoloration that stained its center as I had a hundred times before. A bloody reminder of past victories.

"I'm confused, Sara," the big guy admitted. "What happened here today, the flags, Connor, and now Joel.... I thought we had it all figured out. I thought we were winning this thing."

I sat down next to him and wrapped an arm over his bulging shoulders. "I'm at a loss too," I conceded. "I can't understand how, if we have a guardian angel watching over us, how he would let something like this happen."

"Exactly, right. What the fuck? Worst fucking guardian angel ever." He snickered, despite himself. I smiled, shaking my head.

"What happened up there?" I knew what he was talking about. "Joel isn't the type, is he?"

"I didn't think so, Sonny." I pulled my hair off my face and tied it in a ponytail. "I'm not convinced he did this *himself.*"

Sonny looked at me, confused.

"What I mean is, I don't think he did this freely. I think the drugs, the pressure, and the flags might have had a hand in this." I didn't dare tell him my deepest fear. That Joel couldn't live with himself, that Joel may have deliberately caused Connor's death.

"That adds up. I mean, none of us know what he's been dealing with. Then the *flags* show up and off Connor." His fists tightened into balls. "Glad I got my shot in." Sonny had reacted first when the flags moved in on us, crushing a man's nose with his fist and knocking him unconscious. Connor then pleaded with us not to react. It was as though he knew his fate and didn't want us to suffer similarly.

"Listen, Sonny, don't let Earl talk you guys into something you don't want to do."

"Sara, the *only* thing I want to do right now is wipe them out. All of them. Make them eat that fuck'n flag."

I guess I knew that was coming. I left it alone and went to go back inside.

"He didn't tell you anything, eh?" Sonny raised his voice as I opened the front door. "Joel?"

I froze a moment, not sure how to answer that question.

"You saw what happened, Sonny," I started. "He accused Connor and I of having an affair, then went berserk, hit Connor, and left. You know about as much about where he went and what he was thinking as I do. What are you asking?"

"I'm not sure."

"If you don't have the balls to ask it, then don't *think* it."

He must have known I would defend Joel. I knew what he was asking, it was a terrible thought to entertain, but the motive was there. So was the *letter.*

I moved inside and shut the door behind me.

*****

On my way to Joel's room that same evening, I caught Freddy and Kevin mid-conversation in the hallway. Satisfied they hadn't heard me, I eavesdropped.

"Why wouldn't we follow Earl?" That was Kevin. "Earl knows what he's doing, shit, he *counseled* Joel half the time."

"I'm not against it Kev, I'm not. If I have to make the choice I'll stand behind Earl. Sara's the only other person here to rally behind and I'm not getting behind a girl, Joel's girlfriend or not."

I winced and choked down indignation at Fred's insult. What was worse was that they had already written Joel off. I bowed my head, fiddling with the cup in my hands, fighting to keep my mouth shut.

"That's what I mean, Fred. Sara will have Seth and Caroline on her side for sure, and I'm guessing Sid. I think he and Caroline are sleeping together."

"I'm pretty sure Sonny is behind Earl. He wants revenge on those prick *flags* as much as me."

"Then the house is split. 4/4. How will we have a leader?" Kevin sounded perplexed.

"Well, whatever happens, we're stronger than they are. They couldn't do much to stop us from *taking* control."

Jesus, Earl had his hooks in Fred. I almost dropped the glass in my hand.

"Probably not," agreed Kevin. "Two girls, a *queer* and Sidney."

"Queer?"

"Yeah, pretty sure Seth is *gay*."

"Really?"

"I don't know, probably."

"Whatever. Listen, we'd better get back up to Skylab. You got the movies?"

"Yup. Earl will like these," I could hear the DVD's shake in their boxes as Kevin rattled them. "Lots of blood and guts!"

I listened as they left. It was a terrifying conversation to have overheard. Fred and Kevin had just pledged their allegiance to Earl, calling four friends nothing more than an inconvenience.

Chapter Five

Joel died the following day, making my nightmare complete. We buried him in the backyard, next to Connor. We were experiencing one of the most profoundly distressing periods in our short lives. This was comparable with losing our families in the initial blasts. This was what I'd remembered being lost felt like as a child. Panicked. I had lost my best friend, the man I'd loved - the knowledge that I would never have that back was suffocating me. I couldn't bring myself to be at the funeral. *I wasn't with him.* This was a final regret. I wasn't at his side when he'd passed on. Had he asked for me? Had he spoken at all? I hadn't asked Caroline. She had been with him. All I could feel was grief mixed with envy. She'd seen his final moments. I should never have agreed to sleep. I had exhausted myself with him all night. And so I had missed his final breath.

*****

In the very early hours of the morning, before Joel left me, I had laid with him in bed, under the covers, remembering something I'd said to him once. It was the night before the big fight with Connor. He had been exhausted (high no doubt) but he was lying in bed, looking contented. It was a look of calm.

"I like you best like this," I'd said to him.

"On my back or asleep?"

"Calm. At peace"

He had that look now. No expression passed over his face as I listened to his shallow breathing.

I laid there beside him, stroking his dirty blonde hair, keeping it out of his eyes at first, and then just repeating the motion. I could imagine we were still living the summer months before everything went to hell. We were new, our relationship was in its infancy, but we'd shared so much in such a short time that we could just lay there and not speak. He would indulge me, let me stroke his hair, kiss his shoulder. This usually followed a passionate and impressively lengthy session of lovemaking. I'd only been with one other boy before Joel and that was anything but impressive. Not that I had much experience to draw from, but a girl knows what a girl wants.

At three in the morning Joel spoke once more. It wasn't profound, at least, not at the time. It seemed almost sad that this was what he'd said with his last opportunity to communicate to me. "Go North," he whispered, catching me completely off guard.

"Wha-what?" I whispered back. He did not reply. "Joel…" I sat up, took his head in both my hands and leaned into him. "Joel?" Tears welled up in my eyes and fell on his face. "Say that again," I pleaded. "Say it again, Joel." I lifted his eyelids and stared into his eyes, though they had rolled up into the back of his head. I shook him. "Please… Joel, say that again. Say something, anything. Please!" Realizing he was not going to speak again, I set his head onto the pillow and cried for hours.

*****

The first few days after Joel's passing were numbing. Upon hearing the news from Caroline and falling to my knees, my mind went a mile a minute. I stared at the floor, my unblinking eyes darting back and forth. A hand on my back, meant to comfort me, felt like nothing. I stood and called Caroline a liar. I couldn't grasp that he wasn't coming back, that one evening Joel wouldn't just wake up and turn to me and smile. I wasn't prepared for this. Though I had tried to be logical, understanding that the blood loss, the time spent underwater, and his comatose state did not bode well for his chances, I had convinced myself that his survival was a real possibility.

I charged to the bedroom and stopped short of the door. I stared at Joel on the bed, studying his torso, watching for his chest to rise and fall. They might have been wrong, they might not have checked everything, they weren't doctors. What did they know? I moved to the bed. Had they checked his pulse? Had they listened for his breathing? As the questions ran through my head I pressed my finger to his jugular, and my ear to his mouth, desperate for any sign.

"I tried CPR too, Sara," Seth had followed me as far as the door. I shot a look at him and he stepped back, his eyes falling to the floor.

"Do you even *know* CPR?" I asked spitefully. His hand went up limply and I started the life saving technique, straddling Joel, pushing violently down on his chest, desperate to restart his heart. 1, 2, 3, 4, 5, "Breathe!" I shouted at him. His face was white. I tilted his head, pinched his nose and sealed my mouth around his. I blew hard and long into his lungs, encouraged by the rise in his chest. I repeated the process time and again until after a half hour I was pulled off him, physically exhausted and emotionally crushed.

For days after his burial I replayed his voice in my head, remembering only the good, only the special moments. I couldn't bring myself to think a single negative thought about him. Instead I ran through all the scenarios that would never be. I'd lost everything. He was my every day, in my every thought. How could I survive this place without him? Who would I read to at night? Who would I sleep next to? Who would I share my most intimate thoughts with? The lost opportunities endlessly played out in my mind. I was utterly heart-sick and spent many of the days to follow alone in his room, our room, bed-ridden.

Caroline would visit often and was really the only person I would let in. I let her into my head and into my heart. We'd relive shared memories of Joel and occasionally I would find myself laughing out loud with her as the stories became more ridiculous.

"He was an incredible person," I said, and in saying that aloud, talking about him in past tense, I realized he was gone for good, physically at least. Caroline embraced me as the corners of my smile pulled downward. Caroline was a really good person, someone I wished I'd known better in *life*. She brought me back from the brink, and for that I will be eternally grateful.

I'd decided she would be the first to hear my news, something that would change everything. I had suspected it for months, and I had no way of being entirely certain yet. But sometimes you just know. And I knew.

"I'm pregnant, Caroline," I told her as we sat on the back balcony, taking in a rare afternoon of clear blue skies.

Her mouth opened but no sound came. An expression of fear seemed to pass over her pretty face, a darkness that didn't disappear for some time. Finally, after digesting what I'd told her, and all of its implications, she responded.

"Are you certain? I mean, could you be wrong?" A fair question: it wasn't like we had any pregnancy tests on hand. I hadn't had a period in about two months, but it was more than that. My body felt different -heavier. I felt already a yearning for it. To see this child I could feel growing inside me. I couldn't have been more than 10 weeks along. But already I felt like a mother.

"Yes, I'm sure."

"That's wonderful news, Sara." She smiled, attempting true happiness, despite the circumstances. "Joel's?"

"Yes, of course." I took the defensive. "You didn't believe anything Joel had accused me of with Connor did you?"

"You'd never said either way." She lowered her head. I took her chin in my hand and brought her eyes to mine. "It's Joel's. My God, of course it's Joel's." I shuddered, realizing I was the only one of us alive who could confirm or deny this. "Is that what the others think? Do they think I cheated on Joel with Connor?"

"No, I – I don't know Sara. I shouldn't have asked that. I'm sorry."

"I just don't want there to be any confusion when I tell everyone." I already felt protective of my unborn child.

"Are you sick? What do they call it? Morning sickness?"

"Not really. Not everyone gets that though."

"I guess not." I could tell she wasn't convinced of my state.

"Caroline," I said, smiling. "I'm *pregnant*."

Caroline finally smiled convincingly. The darkness disappeared. "It's great news, Sara."

"Thanks. I'm really scared, but excited too." I stood and paced a moment. Turning to her I felt tears resurfacing. "It feels like an incredible amount of responsibility. And this isn't exactly the best time or place to have a baby."

Caroline stood too and placed her hands on my shoulders, calming my nerves. "People have been having babies in worse places than this. I'll help of course, I'll do whatever you need doing. And you're a med student, or would have been…"

Had the world not taken a turn for the worse, I would have been at one of the finest universities in the country, pre-med. I had been given the opportunity in my final year of high school to co-op with the local hospital where I had witnessed two live births. I just shook my head and hugged her hard. She hugged me back.

Sharing the news had settled me into my new existence. Though I would miss Joel every time I laid my head down to sleep, in every room I entered and every time I looked in the shattered bathroom mirror, I would recover in the knowledge that he would live on in his child. And I would love this child more than I could ever have loved him. I would need to, to make up for the cruelty of bringing a new life into this uncertainty.

While I was making ready for a new life, Earl was making ready for a war.

Chapter Six

A week passed before I shared with Caroline, Sid and Seth what had happened before Joel had died. What he had whispered, impossible as it seemed, in his dying breaths.

"North? Earl and the guys said *not* to go north," reminded Sidney.

After we'd successfully beaten back the flag army, Earl, Sonny and Fred had followed them north to be sure they had travelled far enough, that they would no longer pose a threat to our continued survival. In the time since the bombs fell, several caravans of survivors had passed our fortress. Some we had the opportunity to speak with. All were headed north towards something unknown that was beckoning them on. Their fate became clear when Earl explained what his crew had seen. Two days' march from our position was a vast, mass grave that stretched on for miles. Burnt out vehicles and bodies strewn across the asphalt. They recommended that we not cross that path, that we stay put.

"I don't know why he said it, but that's what he said." I lowered my voice as we had gathered in the kitchen. I drank a glass of the semi transparent water, the well compromised by months of fall-out and radioactive rain early on in the Apocalypse.

"Listen, I'm not sure that's a good idea, going north… what they described was pretty graphic." Seth had a point, but all we had to go on were the words of Earl, Sonny and Freddy, none of whom I held in very high regard anymore.

"There's something I didn't tell you about what he'd said."

"There's more?"

"Not more, just, I don't know, something…"

"Well what, Sara? What is it?" Caroline was frowning.

"It felt like, I don't know, like someone else was speaking through him."

"Like the angel?" Seth interrupted.

"Yes, I mean I wouldn't know what that was like, but there was something about the voice, or the tone or something that just didn't say *Joel* to me." I made a face as I always did after a glass of the dirty water. "What do you guys think? Should we try it?"

"We're still living pretty well here. I don't know if I want to lose that." Seth was right; it might be the dumbest thing we've done, leaving the safety of Joel's house. "Let's see how things work out here over the next little while, then make the decision."

"I'm not excited to leave either; we don't know what's out there," I admitted.

"Should we confront Earl about it?" Caroline stood and opened the fridge, mindlessly panning its limited contents.

"I think we should feel out how things go, like Seth said. Keep this little bit of information to ourselves and make a more educated decision on what to do next."

Sid summed up our situation with three words. "Then we wait."

Chapter Seven

Earl had counted the guns and ammunition and placed them in the addition, save the ones he had hidden around the house. Freddy and Sonny hung on his every word now, while Kevin sat at his right side mimicking Earl's arrogance.

As I approached the four of them in the addition, which had acted as our watch tower for the past nine months – with a clear view of the east, west and north – I heard them discussing their plans once more. It was February and my birthday had just passed, like so many others, unnoticed and unannounced.

"We're still in good shape: the ammunition collected from that last attack really set us up...." Earl was caught off-guard by my entry. I sensed his lingering embarrassment over the hand incident, but it lasted just a moment. He turned to greet me. "Sara, how are you?" False concern. I flinched at the thought of his arms on me – *comforting* me.

"I'm coping," I said. "What's all this?" I waved at the arsenal in front of me.

"Inventory," Sonny offered. He had been sheepish around me since our last conversation. He shouldn't have asked what he did about Joel, and he knew it.

"What brings you by, Sara?" Kevin was at his post at the east windows.

"I want to know what you four are planning. It affects us all."

"Of course it does," Earl broke in, "and it's in all our best interest to support our plan. We can't sit here hoping the flags won't come back."

"So you're going then? *All of you?* Abandoning us here to fulfill some hateful revenge plan?"

"If you could just see it for what it really is, Sara," Kevin jumped in. "This is an important step in securing our futures."

"Is that what Earl's told you?" I glared at him.

"It's what we believe, Sara." Freddy spoke up. "I don't know how you're not getting behind this? You lost Connor *and* Joel."

"*We* lost Connor and Joel." I corrected him. "We all lost a good friend in Connor, and I lost everything when Joel died, and I'm *not* behind this. What does that tell you?"

"You have different ideas of what should be done," answered Earl. "We believe this is what Joel would have wanted."

"Oh, bullshit! Don't drag Joel's name into this. This is what *you* want Earl." I looked accusingly at the other three. "And you've all bought into it."

"It's been decided, Sara. We're going, with or without your blessing." Kevin. What a little prick. I flushed and turned to leave, but thought better of it.

"You do this, and you're separating the house. Seth, Sid, Caroline and I are against it. For the record."

"To each their own," Earl replied.

"I'm pregnant." I don't know why I chose that moment to tell them.

"What?" Freddy was stunned. The other three froze in place. If I could have willed them to remain in that state, we would have all been better for it.

"I'm two months along now, at least." I crossed my arms in front of me.

"Jesus, Sara." The repercussions of this revelation were working their way through Sonny's head.

"That's not good." Kevin's response. Earl slapped Kevin's arm dismissively.

"Joel's?" Earl asked the burning question, licking his thin lips.

"Yes, Jesus Christ, Connor and I weren't…" I felt it was a hopeless argument and just shook my head hard.

"Okay, all the more reason to remove the threat of the flags." Earl faking respect for his fallen leader, and friend, used my news to further his agenda.

"You'll do what you'll do; I just needed to tell you." With that, I left the addition and they returned to their task at hand.

"We leave tomorrow," I heard Earl shout over my shoulder. Part of me hoped they wouldn't return.

Chapter Eight

As we watched them leave, I thought it odd that Caroline hadn't joined us in the front hall to see them off. Seth and Sid shook hands with the four and wished them all the best. No hard feelings.

"We'll watch the house," Sid assured them.

"I know you will, Sid." Earl smiled, his teeth now yellow from the cigarettes. In that moment I wondered how many more they must have. I remembered how Kevin had made finding cigarettes in town a priority.

They left in the Caddy: Joel's father's Cadillac. So many of the vehicles we'd acquired over the months had stopped working, blamed on the weather and lack of maintenance. The caddy had remained in the garage, protected from the elements, and lovingly maintained by Sonny.

"Good riddance," I said aloud.

"Don't say that, Sara." Sid wrapped his arm around me. His touch was soothing. I felt warm and safe but unthreatened, which was the polar opposite to how Earl's touch made me feel. Caroline had told me that he and she had found comfort in each other's arms over the course of the last few weeks, long after John's shooting death in our front hall. She had blamed herself for that, and I knew she'd taken the death of her high school sweetheart terribly.

"I don't know if I mean it or not." I was angry at Earl's ability to just keep going despite everything. I was equally angry at the other three for willingly following Earl so blindly.

"I'm not defending their plan; I think it's flawed. But Earl leads with aggression. You know, he's a 'best defense is a strong offence' type." Sidney had summed Earl up tidily with those words.

"Yeah, I guess I always knew that about him." I turned and put an arm around both Sid and Seth as we walked to the kitchen. "Where is Caroline?"

"I don't know. I woke up alone this morning." Sid admitted.

I was taken aback. "What? Why? Where would she be?"

"Honestly, I thought maybe she'd spent the night with you, talking about your baby, making plans. You know how she likes to make plans." Caroline was gifted at putting things in perspective. She had helped us organize our resources and because of her efforts some of our food and toiletries had outlived their expiry dates.

"Nope, she left my room about midnight last night." We had been talking about the baby, and she had stayed with me until I'd mentioned the time.

"She didn't say where she was heading after that?"

"I didn't ask. I assumed she would have made her way to your room." Sid and Caroline had bunked up in Julia and Connor's old room, across the hall from mine.

"Seth, have you seen Caroline this morning?" Sid pulled away from me while Seth also maneuvered out of my reach.

"I haven't," he said. We all stopped there at the foot of the stairs and looked dumbly at one another. Where was Caroline?

Chapter Nine

We each took a floor to look for Caroline, Sid took the top level, Seth the main floor and I looked in the basement, each of us calling out her name. It was a very large house. Joel's parents had done very well for themselves and built this colossal home in the country. It was an excellent refuge for our original group of fourteen, but full of empty spaces now that we were so few.

Searching the basement I moved through the rooms quickly at first and then slowed down, taking my time, opening closets, although I didn't know why she would be hiding. This was maddening. This was very out of character for Caroline, making it all the more distressing.

After losing hope of finding her in the basement, I opened the door to the cold room where we kept what was left of our canned goods and vegetables from the barn garden. There I found her seated in the fetal position, hugging her knees into her chest, rocking slowly.

"Caroline!" She looked up and I saw a misery in her eyes that stunned me. "What - what's wrong?" My heart sank. The cold room was freezing and smelled of potatoes and dirt.

I approached her quickly, startling her. She pulled away, shivering. I did my best not to touch her; I didn't want to make her worse.

"Oh Caroline, it's freezing in here," I rubbed my arms and looked around. The room was dark: the light from the open doorway made me realize I would have only been a silhouette to her.

"It's Sara, honey. Why are you in here?"

She burst into tears and crawled toward me on all fours. I took her up into my arms and rubbed her back softly. "What's happened?"

She tried to speak, stumbling over her words. She wanted to say so much at once. I hugged her harder, my knees digging into the concrete floor.

"Don't speak, Caroline. Let me take you to Sid."

"No!" She half whispered into my ear. I pulled her back and looked in her eyes. What I saw left me cold.

"What? Why? Tell me what's happened."

"No, not Sid, please, he can *never* know."

"What is it, Caroline? What can he never know?" My skin crawled in anticipation.

"Please, swear to me, you'll never tell him. Never, never." Her face contorted into a twisted, pained look that stayed with me a long time afterward.

"I – I swear," I heard myself say.

Just then Seth and Sid came in. Caroline looked horrified.

"Caroline!" Sid exclaimed. "What are you doing in here?"

"I'm taking her to the shower," I said as I pulled her to her feet. "She's not hurt, Sid, she just needs me right now."

"What's wrong with her?" His voice cracked.

"She's fine Sid, she's uh, had an episode."

"Episode?" He looked confused. I hated lying. I was just trying to protect my friend. Had Sid done something? I couldn't believe that, but why was she so insistent he not know? I was desperate to find out.

"She has them once in a while. Let me through and we'll fill you guys in when we're ready."

"But she's okay? Caroline? You're okay?" He reached for her and she pulled away, using me as a shield.

"She'll be fine, Sid. Seth, you guys just hold down the fort while we work through this."

"What kind of episode are we talking about?" He sounded honestly worried for her. It hurt me to have to avoid his questions; I was making everything up as I went along.

"She's, uh, got a disorder. Just let us through, Sid!" I became more forceful as Caroline's nails clawed into my arm. He and Seth moved aside to let us pass. I smiled and raced with Caroline to the basement bathroom, where I locked the door behind us.

The bathroom had seen better days: it was outfitted with a sauna/shower where I set her down on the cedar bench. Though the sauna hadn't been used since the bombs dropped, it still smelled strongly of damp cedar.

I knelt down in front of Caroline and placed my hands on her cheeks. "What's happened, Caroline? Tell me please."

She sat there shaking as the memories took hold. Though I knew from her state that she had seen or experienced something traumatic, I was not prepared for what she would tell me.

Chapter Ten

Caroline was beside herself. I sat next to her and held her hand. Her grip was crushing. I let her cry until I felt there was an opportunity to ask again.

"What *happened*, Caroline?"

"You don't know," she uttered. "You *can't* know."

"Don't you want to tell me?"

She took in a deep breath and exhaled.

"It was awful…." she said, convulsing at the memories. "I – I don't know *how* to tell you."

"Just take your time, Caroline. I'm here for as long as you need me to be."

She was staring at the tiled floor, her head shaking back and forth. I took a deep breath next, anticipating the news. What could have happened? Had she left the house and seen something so disturbing? Had she had a run-in with someone? The questions were percolating one after another in my mind.

"Promise me you won't tell Sid," she repeated through gasping breaths.

"I promised, Caroline. You know I wouldn't." I wiped her hair from her forehead gently.

She looked up at me and put on a brave face. "Those bastards…." She broke down again, her head shaking from side to side. *Those bastards?* Who was she referring to? Surely not…

"*Earl.*" The name was like a curse coming from her lips.

"What did he *do*, Caroline?" I was beginning to feel sick to my stomach. This wasn't the baby inside me, it was in anticipation of what she would say next.

"He's an evil bastard," she spat out.

"What did he *do*?" A lull in her explanation gave me a chance to breathe again.

"He *raped* me! Okay?! He fucking *raped* me!" she said bluntly, her eyes fixed on me.

I squeezed her hand hard. "Jesus, *what*?"

"*Him*, then Kevin, then - then that *Fred*…" She stopped suddenly, rhyming off the names I would hate forever after. I said nothing more, I only listened. "*Earl* first, cornering me in the kitchen after – after I left your room last night… *was* it last night?" She looked away again trying to focus.

The sauna was the best place in the house to have this secret conversation as it had a heavy wooden door, and the bathroom door itself was shut and locked. If she wanted secrecy, this place would offer it.

"He said he wanted to *kiss* me. He said he'd been *lonely*." She released my hand and placed both hands on her knees, perhaps unconsciously forcing them together. "I told him I wasn't interested. I told him no…" I could see the memories play out on her face, and she frowned deeply. "Please don't tell Sid. Please…" She wept involuntarily and caught her breath. "I'm so *ashamed*."

"*No*," I said automatically. "*No*, Caroline. This is *not* your fault, don't you do that."

"What if I had let him kiss me?" She questioned.

"Goddamn it, Caroline." I was livid. Not with her, but with her thought process. "You are the *victim*."

"He said he was lonely. He said they were *all* so lonely." Jesus Christ, *all of them*, animals! "I – I hate them now." She had every right. I should *kill* them for her, I thought.

Caroline continued to relive the memory. "He took my wrists and pulled me into him, into those yellow teeth… and I *fought* him, I *did*, Sara!" It was crushing to hear the details.

"Then I felt a sharp pain in my stomach." Her hand moved to her midsection.

"I *know*, Caroline." I massaged her shoulder. "And Sid will know that too."

"No! Please don't tell him, Sara." I wanted to so he would take matters into his own hands and kill that fuck. All of them. But I'd promised.

"Okay, Caroline, I won't. If that's really what you want, I will keep my promise." It ate me up inside, but maybe she'd change her mind in time.

"He dragged me to the basement by the neck, I – I couldn't scream or speak." She was stone-faced now. "I tried to wiggle free, but he was too strong. When we reached the bottom of the stairs I knew I was in trouble. He kept dragging me across the floor and I went limp. I thought maybe my dead weight would make it harder but he kept going. Then he threw me on the couch and I said I would scream and he hit me in my face." A hand moved slowly to her temple where I guessed Earl had punched her.

"Jesus Christ, Caroline. I'm so sorry." I stroked her hair. I wanted to make it better for her. I thought briefly how this could have been me.

Tears burned my eyes and I rubbed them out. I felt I needed to be strong for her. She continued her story saying that Kevin and Fred had followed. The attack had clearly been planned in advance. Tears rolled down both of our cheeks. Had they only spared me because of my pregnancy? What if I hadn't revealed this the day before? A full-body shiver went through me. How had it come to this?

"But they were drunk; I could smell the gin on their breath, in my ear. Maybe if they weren't drinking…"

"Jesus, Caroline." I managed through my hoarse throat. "Don't give them anything. They did it, that's enough. Don't give them *anything*."

"I don't know how long I laid there. I don't even know how I ended up in the cold room. I just knew I couldn't face any of them."

"Where was Sonny during all this?" I asked, propping myself up.

"Never heard his voice."

"Sons of bitches." I growled through clenched teeth. I vowed I would kill them then and there. The how and the when would eventually present themselves.

Chapter Eleven

The night Earl, Fred, Kevin and Sonny left to chase the flags, I found myself in the addition with Seth, trying to keep busy while we kept watch - as we had countless times before. It was a chore, one which I'd always dreaded. The boredom of sitting alone and staring out the windows, often into an abyss of blackness, was numbing. When the clouds dominated the skies and there were no stars, moon or even a faint flicker of light in the distance to focus on, your shift, in what we had nicknamed Skylab, seemed doubly painful. Of course, with the absence of light, seeing the enemy was made all the more easy, as they would carry either a torch or a flashlight, something to light their way in the darkness.

This night did not produce an enemy, thankfully. Nor was the sky as black as it once was. Clouds moved slowly, offering us a glimpse of a star or even the moon. It was waxing Gibbous that night. Gibbous, a term I had learned recently, in one of Joel's childhood books. Having read virtually every book in the house, I had turned to purely educational reading, and then finally to educational children's books. I liked to think of the moon waxing rather than waning; the idea it would reveal itself gave me hope. Watching it wane made me feel as though it would disappear again, as it did in the beginning, and maybe forever this time.

While poking around in Earl's things - he and the other three had taken to sleeping in the addition - I came across a booklet under a pillow, a journal of sorts. It was one of Kevin's sketch books, with a black textured cover and about 200 bright white pages. Many of these pages had been filled with a very steady hand. The penmanship was impressive. It was Earl's handwriting;

I recognized it immediately from his maps and charts and timetables which he'd posted around the house.

After thumbing through the pages I closed the book, my interest falling back to the cover which had been carved with a knife. The carving formed words, and the words alarmed me for several reasons.

MY STRUGGLE

The title itself told a story. But knowing Earl, and relating the title to a history lesson on the Discovery Channel a few years back, MY STRUGGLE became profoundly more disturbing when translated into German; *Mein Kampf.* Hitler's autobiography, and political ideology which propelled him into his role in infamy. Knowing Earl, he knew exactly how this title translated, and to whom he would be comparing himself. How would I live with someone I hated, someone I wanted dead? I opened the journal again and read, suddenly feeling Seth's eyes upon me.

"Are you sure you should be reading that, Sara?" he questioned timidly.

"What's the harm? They won't be back for days."

"What did Caroline say to you today when you found her?" he asked, changing the subject.

"She's fine, Seth," I lied. In fact, I wondered if she'd ever be fine again. "She had an episode." I was sticking with that answer. People seemed to stop asking when you said the word 'episode'.

"Okay." He let it go and I started flipping pages, hoping to gain some advantage over Earl by reading his secret thoughts.

"I was impressed more than anything with the way Gareth carried himself. The total control he had over his membership inspired me." He referred to the leader of the flags, who had hoped to grill each of us in an attempt to weed out supposed 'sympathizers' to the Reaper's ideals. Gareth was a small man, and he ruled with fear. Joel saw that.

I read on. *"Gareth was well spoken, superior in his demeanor. People need to be led. People need to feel safe. Gareth offered those things. Two things to rule: offer safety and offer leadership."* He was taking notes the whole time!

"Leadership is often thrust upon an individual. Joel was voted our leader, and Joel cracked under the pressure. What is better is to take leadership, there is power in that and people respect power." I felt a pang of anxiety. He was building himself up to lead us all, and he would *take* control. As I read on, I found more passages that related to leadership; entire pages filled with plans to lead an army of his own, schematics of battles we'd fought. He took nothing for granted. He learned from everything and he documented it. I'd said before that Earl was

too intelligent to have such a scary side. The very idea of Earl in control made me sick with fear.

Flipping through more of the text I stopped again at a section entitled; **Sexual cleansing - the immediacy of procreation.** *"The purpose of life is to procreate and evolve. In a world where humanity has likely lost most of its populace, procreation is key to the survival of the species. What does not encourage procreation cannot be allowed to consume resources. A sexual cleansing is necessary. The homosexuals need be exposed and exterminated, so as not to consume that which will feed humanity's future."*

"So, whose journal is it? Kevin's?" Seth sounded despondent. My heart went out to him. I knew he was gay, I'd always known, and reading Earl's grand plan, I wondered if he knew it too.

"No, Earl's," I replied and cleared my throat. Should I show him? I felt I had to protect him.

"So, what's he saying? Kill the flags - good. Hate your neighbor – good. No more ammo – bad. Something along those lines?"

I laughed and smiled at him, then shook my head.

"He's fucked, Seth, and I'm afraid we're in trouble. He's talking about taking control, leading us all."

Seth didn't like the sound of that. "Earl can go fuck himself. The guy's a pussy with a gun. I'd never follow him."

"But what if he used the others to back him up? We're two women and two men. He's got four men."

"Well, I can't see those guys actually forcing us to do something. I mean Jesus, we're all friends here right?"

I thought of what they'd done to Caroline and almost used it as an example but stopped myself.

"I think they're all under his spell and are capable of anything. The most we can hope for now is that the flags get to them before they get to the flags." And I meant it. They would be doing us a favor if they killed Earl. I feared for our futures and for the future of my baby if he returned.

Chapter Twelve

Earl, Sonny, Fred and Kevin returned to the house a week later. My heart sank at the sight of them. One, two, three, four, I counted as they moved through the front door, no worse for wear as far as I could tell. Sonny went straight to the kitchen, passing me without a word.

"What happened?" I asked, struggling to contain my hatred.

"We got them," Fred said on his way to the basement. I became nervous: they were all behaving strangely.

"Well, is something wrong?" I asked.

"Nothing to concern yourself with." Kevin marched past me, following Sonny into the kitchen.

"You fucking pussies!" Earl cried from the front hall. I jumped out of my skin. I flushed at the sight of him.

"Rest easy, Sara." Mistaking my rage for fear, he approached me. "We got *all* of 'em!" While he spoke, he flapped a piece of *something* between his fingers. He also wore a colored cape draped over his shoulders.

"Oh my God." As he got closer I could see what he held. It was *skin*, flesh! I backed off automatically. *"What have you done!"*

"This is my *prize!*" he shouted. "All of ours! Think of it as *our* flag, courtesy of *the* flags!" Then he removed the cape from around his shoulders, threw it over the railing of the staircase and went to the kitchen. I was frozen in terror at what I was seeing.

*****

That night, I couldn't sleep. The mental image of human flesh draped across the railing just one floor beneath me was too horrifying for words. I could only imagine what my subconscious would conjure up if I allowed myself to sleep. I had seen so much death by this point, nothing should have shocked me. But this blatant desecration incurred a new level of horror. Finally, when I could toss and turn no more, I got up and wandered outside, escaping through the bedroom window, crossing the rooftop and navigating down the TV antenna to where Sonny was standing on the back patio.

Chapter Thirteen

"Talk to me, Sonny." I begged him. "Whose skin *is* that?"

"It's Gareth's," he replied. "*Jesus*, Sara..." His head lowered and his eyes closed.

"I don't think I want to know any more."

"We killed them all. We killed most of them in their sleep. But when the guns went off a few of them woke up, and we shot them down." He paused. "Maybe to them it was all a dream, you know? Doesn't everyone hope they'll just die in their sleep?"

"Yeah," I said, mesmerized by the monotone of his voice.

"We shot them like cattle. One, two, three... they fell like sacks of potatoes, blood everywhere." Judging from his tone, Sonny had realized revenge wasn't all it was cracked up to be.

"I wish you hadn't gone, Sonny."

He turned then and looked at me wearily. "Yeah. Me too, Sara."

He continued to describe how Freddy had located Gareth during the early part of the melee and secured him to a tree with rope, letting him watch his army be gunned down in front of him. Earl swaggered over to Gareth when the last of his followers were dead, and before cutting his throat, said; "Ever seen an animal *skinned*, Gareth? Know how many animals *I've* skinned? Enough to know how to skin a man." Then the knife came out and Earl slid it across Gareth's throat slowly, a shallow cut. Thick red blood ran slowly down his neck and chest, collecting on his robe. The cut was not deep enough to kill, only to torture. Gareth's mouth opened as if to protest and Earl jabbed the knife down on his tongue cutting through his jaw. He left it there for a time and circled his victim, sizing him up.

Michael E. Poeltl

Finally, after facing the leader of the flag army once more, Earl pulled his sidearm and shot Gareth in the head, just as Connor had been executed. Freddy then untied Gareth and Earl went to work on the corpse.

"*Jesus*, Sonny," I choked. "That's horrifying."

"Yeah, pretty fucking sick."

"What are we going to do about him?" He knew who I meant: Earl.

"I don't know anymore." He was distraught. "I'm not taking sides. I'm leaving."

He said he wanted to resume his long-abandoned search for Tom, a friend who we'd lost during those first crucial hours after the bombs had dropped. Tom was a gawky looking kid, his eyes too big for his face, his teeth misshapen and his self-esteem non-existent. Sonny was looking for purpose again, some semblance of reason to go on. I pleaded with him to stay, to watch over me and the baby.

"Sonny, I - I'm so sorry things between us got so messed up. But you see now, you *see* what Earl is. He's sick!"

"I see that. I guess I always knew that, Sara. But after Connor, and Joel…." He trailed off. "After the flags and everything went to shit, after all we'd accomplished here. I just needed someone to tell me it was alright to take revenge."

I placed a hand on his shoulder. "Sonny, I'm scared for us. I *need* you to stay." I wiped away a tear with my other hand.

Sonny gently removed my hand. "Sara, I'm *not* staying. I *can't*."

"I'm begging you, Sonny." I began to cry. "He'll kill us all, eventually. He'll write a reason in his journal and then he'll carry it out." Sonny's heavy hand touched my head gently.

"There's nothing for me here, Sara."

I couldn't argue that there was nothing here, but what was there *beyond* here? Part of him had died when Connor and Joel died, the other part perished during that trip he had taken with Earl to exact revenge. We were all dying inside. How much more could any of us take? I resigned myself to his departure.

"Come with me." He suggested.

"Where would we go?" I asked.

"East. Tom had family on the east coast. And then we could find a boat. And then…"

"And then?"

"Then we'll sail it." He turned to look at the house and breathed deeply. Looking back at me his gaze lingered. "You're not coming, are you, Sara?" He smiled sadly then.

A journey like that was not something I could manage while pregnant. Open to the elements, food and shelter uncertain from day to day. "I'll miss you, Sonny."

"Don't," he said, before he turned and entered the house for the last time. I would never see Sonny again.

Chapter Fourteen

Caroline had not recovered from the attack, and her deep depression left Sid with little to work with.

"I don't know what's going on, Sara. Caroline won't so much as let me touch her. Has she said anything to you?" Sid sat with me on the edge of my bed, where I huddled and fought back pregnancy-related nausea.

"The episode." I kept up the lie. "She's still shaken from her *episode* last week. She'd never experienced anything like that before and she's afraid it could happen again." I was becoming an excellent liar. Not something I was particularly proud of, but necessary to keep a promise to a friend.

"I can't seem to reason with her and it's scaring me you know? I feel like Connor must have felt when Julia was so depressed." Our friend Julia, a former resident of this home and my very best friend, had cut her own wrists months ago to avoid bringing a child into this world. This memory haunted me more than ever, having now become pregnant myself and experiencing the same sad thoughts.

"Sidney, give her some time. I'll continue to talk with her, you just be her rock until she can open up to you again."

"I guess. I miss her though."

"I know you do. I miss the old Caroline too. Be patient, okay?"

"I will. Thanks, Sara." Sid left me to my thoughts. I was sitting up in bed, caressing my ever expanding stomach. What would my baby look like, I wondered. God I hoped it would be healthy. Who knew what the last few months could do to a fetus. I put those thoughts out of my mind and decided he would be a he, and that he would look like Joel. Ten fingers, ten toes, bald, and terribly handsome. I smiled and realized I was looking forward to meeting him. But what would I call him? I had no names picked. Should I call him Joel after his father? No, I decided that would be too painful. Maybe I'd name him after my own father, Leif. That was a strong name, and he would need all the strength he could get.

Just then Kevin appeared at my door. "Sara," he said flatly, "Earl would like your ear."

"Then tell Earl to come see me. I'm not jumping every time he calls."

"I'll let him know."

I wasn't looking forward to facing Earl one on one. We were used to arguing with each other now over just about everything, but in front of everyone, never just the two of us. I felt an urge to get up and call Sid back into the room when Earl's frame blocked the doorway.

Chapter Fifteen

"Earl." I greeted him uncomfortably. His hands were hanging from the top of the door frame and his feet jammed up against either side of the opening as if to fill the space completely.

"Sara. Can we talk about this baby of yours?"

"I see no reason to discuss that with you," I shot back.

"No reason? I'm the one protecting this house; you have every reason to discuss this with me."

"We're *all*, all of us protecting this house, Earl. Not just you!"

"Sara. Who's in charge here? Who in your mind is leading this group now?"

"Not you."

"Oh, no? Then who? Who lives in Skylab, keeping watch day and night?"

"That's your choice to live there. The rest of us are doing our part too."

"Let's not just agree to disagree this time, Sara. I need you to acknowledge my leadership so we can move forward." He motioned toward me, trying to intimidate me. I wasn't scared of Earl, though maybe I should have been after what he did to Caroline and Gareth. But, for some reason, Earl was still just Earl to me, my boyfriend's sycophant.

"You won't get that out of me, Earl."

"Why do you hate me so much, Sara? Why, after all I've managed to accomplish here, why do you *hate* me so much?" His voice lowered to a menacing hiss.

"Are you kidding, Earl? You know *exactly* why I hate you. You, Kevin and Fred." His eyes narrowed as he understood.

"So, you know." He stood upright and his hands shot down to his sides. "Get over yourself, you little bitch! She wanted it! And that's between her and me."

My eyes widened and he knew he'd said the wrong thing to the wrong person. He took a step back as I got to my feet. I slammed my open palms against his chest and shoved him out the door. "You just pray I don't tell Sid and Seth. Caroline asked me to promise. But I'm rethinking the whole thing now."

"Careful, Sara. You be careful what you say to who." His finger was in my face. I slapped it away. "I'm the leader of this group now," he hissed through clenched teeth. "You get comfortable with it. Disrespect me again and I'll show you what it is to go against me."

I slammed the door and paced. I could hear the addition door slam also. I fanned my face and sat on the bed, breathing deeply and exhaling slowly. We had to remove Earl altogether. But how?

Chapter Sixteen

W e spent the ensuing months tending the barn garden, collecting seeds from the plants and replanting them. This garden had been nothing less than a miraculous discovery during the early days after the Reaper had struck. In the midst of all of the chaos, we discovered a barn facility, untouched by the fall out, complete with hydroponics equipment and a lifetime of marijuana. What had been someone's (perhaps the government's, based on the size and level of operation) enterprise had become our lifesaver. We had replaced the marijuana with vegetable seeds we'd scavenged from hardware and department stores, and began using the barn garden as a source for fresh vegetables and fruit. The barn had a similar setup to Joel's house, boasting a private well to feed the crop and a generator that ran on the same fuel we used at the house. Without the hydroponic garden we would surely have suffered a bout of scurvy or worse, seeing how the last of our canned fruits and veggies had been consumed within the first year. At just a few minutes' drive from the house on the ATV, the barn was a welcome change of pace from the stresses at home.

When I wasn't in the barn garden, helping out, sorting seeds or checking hoses I'd spend time alone, usually in the bathroom adjacent to Joel's room, staring into the shattered mirror as my hand gently caressed my baby bump.

More often than not I would cry. Not because my pregnancy upset me, or that my hormones were getting the better of me, but because I missed Joel, my baby's father. That the baby would grow up without a dad made me anxious. Then again, if he *had* survived, what irreparable damage would he have suffered and how would his pain translate to his child? Jesus, I was studying myself in the very mirror he'd smashed the night he chose to take his own life.

The bump had grown slowly in the last couple of months. With these limited resources, I didn't have the privilege of eating whatever I craved. Had that been the case, I was sure I would have been bigger by now. Still, I tried to eat as well and as often as I could and the size of my belly had proven that my attempts at proper nutrition were at least growing something in there.

Nothing made me happier than feeling my baby move. It was a constant source of relief for me. In our present circumstances, with no vitamins and barely any meat products save the recent stash of jerky Earl had found in an abandoned trailer, my diet consisted of berries, lettuce, and canned beans for the most part. Feeling the baby move inside me was an experience I often enjoyed alone. I would think of Joel then as well. Imagining his hand on my belly, with mine guiding his to the kicks and punches.

Six months into my pregnancy (or so was my best guess), I was really showing. My lower back ached even when I sat down. Caroline remembered her stepsister lying on her side with a pillow between her legs when she was pregnant years before. I gave it a shot, and it did help some in relieving the constant pressure.

"Thanks, Caroline."

"Anything I can do to help!" Mercifully, Caroline had come around a couple of months ago. We had a real breakthrough session that put a smile back on her face and love back into her heart. Sid was thankful. He had endured a lot those past months and with little to no explanation as to why. He was an excellent boyfriend.

Seth, to his great shame, had slipped on something in the kitchen and bruised his tailbone on the tile. He was mostly couch-ridden, seated on a collection of pillows to keep him from resting directly on his bruise. We watched movie after movie on DVD together, me pregnant and him an invalid. I loved Seth, and he loved spending time with me. I would say that our time together those days meant more to me than he could ever imagine.

Unfortunately, despite the good times spent with Caroline, Sid and Seth, things had remained as tense as ever with Earl. I was wondering how much more of him I could bear, and carefully weighing my options.

He and his group remained in Skylab, caressing their guns and counting their bullets. They'd moved a TV and DVD player up to the addition as well. We'd split the movies, seeing each other only in passing or to swap one film for another.

I knew eventually I'd need to make a move. But for now, I let my body do its work. The life growing inside me was all that mattered. I almost couldn't believe it was a real human being alive inside me. I longed for an ultrasound, if only to prove to myself that it was really happening, although the occasional kick to my ribs or organs assured me it was. Still, without an image or face, I already felt the inherent need to protect my child, this little person was a part of me. So I waited. And I grew.

*****

I was getting a little stir-crazy at what I'd decided was nearing the seventh month of my pregnancy. My belly seemed to have dropped dramatically in the past week and I'd felt a greater stress on my hips. I was honestly *waddling* around the house, legs bowing as though to clear a path should the baby decide at any moment to drop out of me.

"We're heading to the garden, Sara. You good here with Seth?" Sidney and Caroline were dressing for the strangely cool weather in the front hall.

"Actually, mind if I come along?"

"Not at all. Is Seth good here on his own?"

"I can't see why not." I stepped into the family room. "Seth, mind if I go to the barn with these two? I need an escape for a couple of hours."

"You're going to miss the movie!" he shouted from his plush throne. I smiled at him. "Go on." He waved me away. "We've both seen it like, 10 times in the past year. I'm good."

"Thanks, Seth. We won't be long, honest, and then we'll watch it again, okay?" I laid a hand on his shoulder and he reached up with his, before I followed the other two out of the house. I hopped on the ATV and we pushed out across the field towards the barn.

The bumpy ride over the hardened dirt wasn't exactly a good idea, but Sid took it slow. The sun would set in a couple of hours so we'd try to get in and out within a reasonable time, so not to have to navigate the dark.

Once inside we pushed on with our chores but all the while I was feeling guilty for having left Seth on his own, in that house, with Earl, Kevin and Fred there to bully him. Suddenly, and for whatever reason that passage from Earl's notebook popped into my head, and reminded me why I might be feeling uneasy over leaving him on his own.

Chapter Seventeen

The trip back through the field on the ATV left me terribly anxious. I was convinced something awful was unfolding back at the house. At my insistence we pulled up to the front door and rushed inside.

"Seth!" I called as we poured into the front hall. "Seth, are you in here?" No answer. Then an ache struck my abdomen, travelling from one side to the other and back again. I fell to my knees from the pain, Sid and Caroline on either side of me.

"Is it the baby, Sara?" asked Sid as he helped me up.

"Of course it's the baby," Caroline said as she held my other arm. "It could come any time now."

"Do you want to lay down, Sara?" Sid was practically dragging me to the living room.

"Sure." I felt too weak to argue. "Can you please look for Seth?"

"Sure, Sara, Sid will look for him and I'll stay with you," Caroline soothed while Sid left the room.

"If they've done anything to Seth…." I screeched through the pain.

"I'm sure he's fine." Caroline helped me recline on the couch. "Is this a contraction, do you think?"

"Maybe." I doubled over again and grasped my belly. "Oh, shit, Caroline it hurts like hell."

"I think you might be having that baby."

"Get me upstairs."

Caroline slowly assisted me up the stairs to Joel's room.

"I want Seth! Where is Seth!" It sounded pathetic, but I couldn't help myself. Pain and anxiety were tearing me apart.

"Don't panic, Sara."

"Get me boiled water and towels, Caroline, and scissors and something to clamp off the umbilical." These were some of the things I'd trained myself to ask for when the big moment arrived.

Sidney appeared a second later. "The entire house is empty, I-" he stopped himself. "Shit, are you having that baby?" He looked scared to death. Was it the current situation or something else? Again the pain struck. Such pressure. All other thoughts and concerns flew from my mind. I concentrated on the pressure and my breathing. I couldn't believe it was going to happen. I knew from experience these things usually took much longer to progress, especially with a first child, and I was worried at the close proximity of the contractions to one another. Maybe something was wrong. But this baby wanted out, immediately.

"She's having her baby," Caroline hissed excitedly as she rushed past him with the pot of water and towels in hand. We had decided earlier that we wouldn't tell the others when the birth was taking place. I didn't want any of them involved, so we'd made this pact to do it alone. I looked again for Seth, the only other person I wanted to see right now, but there was no sign of him. Just Sidney standing awkwardly in the hall, the blood draining from his face.

"Jesus, *really*, Sara? Isn't this early?" he wondered aloud.

"I think so, but then, what do I know?" I moaned. The pain was just bearable. I knew it would become increasingly worse as the night went on, and from the way the first contractions felt, I wasn't looking forward to the big ones!

"Wow, Sara…" Caroline was so happy for me, for us, it made me weepy. My hormones had been all over the place the last week as well. Perhaps I should have known this would happen sooner rather than later. Where was Seth? He'd been my rock through so much of my pregnancy. I summoned the memory of his kind smile and voice repeating, *"It'll be okay. Everything will be fine"*.

The labor went on for most of the night. Caroline read anxiously through the same pages of a medical textbook I'd perused countless times the past few months. Sid was in and out of the bedroom repeatedly throughout the night to check on whether anyone had resurfaced. Each time he reported the same news. No one. The rest of the house was empty.

"Check my dilation again, Caroline" I begged as the pain worsened. She lifted the blankets and placed her gloved finger inside me. I knew this was hard for her, but I think she appreciated just how much harder it was for me.

"I don't know, Sara, it feels somewhere between a cheerio and the hole of a bagel, maybe seven centimeters? Three more and you're good to go." Her head shot back to the closed door where Sid stood guard. "What was that?" she whispered to him.

"I'll check it out. Try to be quiet."

We'd all heard it. A door had slammed; maybe the front door. Sidney closed the bedroom door behind him. We listened as he descended the stairs to the front hall. Caroline looked back at me.

"I'm sure it's nothing," she said. "You're doing *great*, Sara. I bet you'll have this baby out in a couple of hours."

It had been six hours already, and honestly, I didn't know how much longer I could keep this up without screaming. The pain of the contractions had increased enormously, and I dreaded the actual pushing. I had almost asked Caroline to light me the pipe, Joel's pot pipe, to take the edge off, but never did. Women had been delivering babies for ages before pain relievers became the delivery room standard. I could do it, but I would have to be strong, stronger than I'd ever been before.

Another violent burning sensation forced my back to arch as I let out a pained cry. Jesus, would it ever let up? Caroline tried to sooth me.

"Is there anything more I can do to help? Do you want a couple of aspirin?"

"Thins the blood," I said automatically. I'd already reviewed all of my options in pain management and none that we had on hand offered any relief for childbirth. The pot would be my best choice, but I didn't want to bring my baby into the world *high*. Since Joel's descent into madness or depression or both, I'd been very careful to stay away from the stuff too.

Sid reappeared a moment later. "I don't see anyone, anywhere." He looked alarmed as well as confused.

"Let's not worry about them. We've got a long night ahead of us," Caroline urged.

"I don't think I can do this," I cried through heavy breaths. "It's too painful."

"You *can* do this, Sara, you *are* doing it, and we'll be right here every step of the way." I caught a look of passing panic in her eyes, but that was quickly replaced with a steely stare that evoked a quiet confidence. I was in good hands, but wished I could be on both sides of the action.

"Sid, take Sara's hand," she ordered in a whisper. Sid rounded the bed and sat next to me. I grabbed at his right hand and squeezed down hard as another contraction overtook me.

The evening turned into night and still, no baby. At roughly midnight the pushing began. "I have to push!" I pleaded. "I have to!"

"You're fully dilated, Sara." Caroline smiled triumphantly and removed her finger once more. "PUSH!" she urged. "PUSH!"

I brought my legs up to my chest, pulling them against my sides with both arms, my muscles straining as I pushed with all my might. Sid was standing next to me, silently patting my forehead with the same wet towel I'd been sucking on to stay hydrated while Caroline coached me. I forgot my earlier resolve to keep the procedure secret, and openly cursed, shouted, ranted and hated the whole experience. My sheets were absolutely soaked in sweat, I was dehydrated and beginning to worry after the first hour whether this baby was going to require a C-section. I put that thought out of my mind, as no one here could perform that with any level of success. Any attempt would definitely kill me, and likely the baby. Not that either of my friends could have brought themselves to cut me open. This was going to happen the old fashioned way, no ifs, ands or buts about it.

Suddenly Caroline declared that she could see the head. A wave of relief overtook me, offering a reprieve from the painful work. That my baby wasn't facing the other way gave me cause for thanks.

"Lots of hair," she noted, sweat glistening on her face as she looked up at me from her position between my legs. "Could be a girl!" But I knew it was a boy.

From the moment she announced the appearance of his head, it was just a few more minutes of pushing before my baby was born.

It was two hours to the minute, five months to the day that Joel had left me. A bittersweet birthday, that his son should be born on the day his father passed away into the dark, forever.

The baby cried as Caroline struggled to cut the cord and clean him off. Thank God he was healthy. If he'd required any medical assistance he might not have made it past his first day.

"Seven months." Sid recalled the brief length of my pregnancy, looking incredulously at the new life in my arms. "Lucky number." We all smiled. In fact, I couldn't will the smile off my face. I stared at the tiny baby in my arms with a love that could not be spoken. A little me. A little *Joel*.

The placenta came out moments after. It was a bizarre thing to behold, resembling a giant organ, with delicate, dark veins running through it.

Caroline pulled it gently with the umbilical cord. This part too was painful, but after the relief of finally having the baby out of me, I pushed bravely through my tears of happiness.

I was lucky: no tearing. He was small enough at just seven months not to have done any collateral damage to his mother.

I spent the rest of the day in bed, recuperating, drinking fluids, tended to by Caroline. The baby, Leif, as I'd named him, after my father, rested comfortably beside me. Lucky again to have a healthy baby boy that even at one or two months premature had no trouble breathing. I wondered that something so small and helpless could be alive. But there he was. His eyes opened briefly and although I knew he could only make out shapes at this age, it was as though we made eye contact. He knew, and I knew, we were both in this together. I had brought a new life into this crazy world, one that depended on me for its very survival. And survival was top-of-mind for all of us. With that in mind, I set my sights on feeding him. With no formula for him, I knew it was breast milk or bust. I brought his tiny head to my left breast, expecting him to latch on immediately. Instead, he turned his face away and began to cry.

Each time I put him to my breast, his tiny mouth was unable to navigate my nipple.

"This isn't working," I said to Caroline, frustrated. "He's not getting *anything* to eat." I was becoming frantic.

"We'll get there, Sara. He's going to have to take it eventually."

My mind suddenly wandered to thoughts of Seth. "Has Sid located anyone yet? Seth?"

"No. It's really weird, right? None of them."

"Why would Seth go off with those animals?"

"I don't know." A shared fear mounted between us as we came to the same conclusion. I shook my head and pulled my baby a little closer to my face.

"Sid will find him, Sara. Just concentrate on Leif." She got up from her seated position on the bed beside me and left the room, closing the door softly. With Leif nestled firmly in my arms, I fell asleep, exhausted, but deeply in love.

*****

Sid was out of breath and soaked to the bone. Caroline was trailing as they entered my bedroom. He had found Seth and confirmed the return of the others to Skylab.

"I'm so sorry, Sara." He pushed the hair out of my face, kneeling at my bedside. His hands were hot, but wet. Instantly I knew what had happened. Seth was dead. I would never see him again. Another bloody senseless tragedy. Just as one little life was beginning another had ended. What had I done? Why had I brought a child into this madness? I closed my eyes and wept openly. Caroline lifted the baby out of my arms and handed him to Sid. She crawled in next to me and hugged me until my convulsive, breathless weeping exhausted us both and sleep overcame us. But just as I was about to drift off, I tried Leif once again at my breast. He took it in his tiny mouth, and sucked for dear life. It was do or die for all of us now. Perhaps he sensed this too.

Chapter Eighteen

The next morning Sidney shakily related the gruesome discovery of Seth. After searching fruitlessly within the house he had decided to try the forest behind the backyard, toward the shed. Grave markers of friends long since dead gave him an eerie feeling of dread as he continued past them. It was dark, but the moon was occasionally granted an audience as the dense groupings of clouds moved swiftly by. As Sidney approached the outer reaches of our property, he heard a strange sound. Though the wind had picked up considerably, he hadn't noticed the trees bending in any noticeable fashion. The sound became louder the closer he moved toward the shed. It resembled the sound you might experience if you were sitting on a tire swing, gently moving yourself back and forth on your heels as the rope stretched and pulled against a large branch of a tree. At least, that's how Sidney described it. For a long moment Sid stood listening, his semi-automatic poised, but the sound just kept on, lethargic in its repetition. He continued, slowly, cautiously on the path he had started.

The clouds backed off, bathing the forest in light just as Sid realized what was producing the eerie sound. As we hadn't seen rain in over a week, a sudden breeze picked up dust from the forest floor, filling Sid's eyes with the grit. He raised his arms to protect his face from the stinging needles and debris caught up in the abrupt wind storm. But as quickly as it had come, it left. Sid wiped his eyes with both hands, his weapon slung over his shoulder, his eyes tearing up, blindly walking along the beaten path. Having walked the path a hundred times, both in *life* and in our post-Apocalyptic present, he knew every step and could navigate the way safely, blindfolded, on a bet. But something startled him as he bumped into a foreign object impeding his progress to the shed.

He immediately backed off, opening his blurry eyes, blinking away the remaining grit, rifle pulled out in front of him.

As his vision began to return he realized the object was suspended in space, hanging from one of the larger trees in the middle of the path. The object was not a fallen branch. It was Seth, rope attached to his neck.

Sidney spun around, blinking madly, searching the darkness for those responsible. Were they watching him? Was he next?

There was little doubt in his mind as to who had done this. But why? Seth would never have done this to himself.

With the wind came the rains, hard and falling fast. It would last only a few minutes, but long enough to turn the hardened soil into a mucky mess, exacerbating Sidney's desperate effort to ascend the hill and protect his friends.

Chapter Nineteen

The following day I made up my mind. They *needed* to die. They had murdered Seth. They could not be allowed to hurt us, or especially my baby. Sid checked on Skylab and confirmed our three enemies were now sitting quietly, drinking what remained of the alcohol and smoking what little weed was left. We went to work immediately. They were too proficient with their weapons, and I was afraid if a gun fight ensued we'd lose. So, I'd decided to torch the house that night. First we'd pack our gear, food and water and lay it out behind the pool for easy retrieval. How it had come to this I couldn't say. These strangers had been my friends. We had relied on one another during the most difficult time in our lives. But something had happened to them. Something had snapped in their brains. Like undomesticated animals, they had allowed their instinctual selves to take over in survival-mode. Perhaps the same thing was happening to me. Like a lioness protecting her cubs, I would stop at nothing to see no more harm came to those I loved, those I had left. They had to die.

"Where will we go?" Sid asked.

"North," I said confidently. "That's the plan. That's where I'm going, with Leif."

"*We're* going wherever *you're* going, Sara." Caroline confirmed, and it was done. We would go north, as Joel had instructed in his unconscious state, on his death bed.

After the provisions were bagged and stashed under cover of darkness, we barricaded both the house and the garage doors, locking them in. They were blissfully unaware of our intentions as we carried out my orders, using old food tins to pour fuel from the tanker around the perimeter of the house. I even dumped a can on the Caddy and whispered an apology to Joel's absent father. We then moved inside the house and carefully spilled the fuel up and down the central staircase. Sid had suggested this: *the more that ignites immediately the less chance they have of making it out.* With that logic in mind, I continued to pour the contents of the tanker throughout the house. I wanted to be doubly sure they didn't make it out.

As I entered the kitchen I heard a door swing open on the second floor, and froze. I heard laughing and then Kevin complained about a smell.

"Why does it smell like *lighter fluid* or gasoline or something up here?"

Jesus, this wasn't going to work. I thought they had smoked themselves to sleep.

"Close the fucking door," I heard Fred shout at him.

"No really, there's a *smell* out here."

"Then go see what it is." That was Earl. I was still standing stock-still in the kitchen, afraid my plan was now in tatters. If Kevin came down the stairs he'd surely notice they were wet, and put it together.

"What *is* that?" He was at the top of the stairs now and coming down. "What the *fuck*…" Shit. This was it, he was going to report back to the others and-

"Kevin." It was Sid. Oh, thank God. Sid was coming up from the basement.

"Sid, you *smell* that?"

"Yeah, man. Come here, I want to show you something."

"You know what this is? Should I get Earl?" They met in the front hall.

"Do you need to bother Earl?" Sid played him perfectly.

Kevin glanced up the curving stairs and shrugged his narrow shoulders. "Guess not."

"Are the others up in Skylab?"

"Yeah, man. What's the *deal*, Sid?" Kevin lifted his bare foot and wiped away the fuel. "Is this what I *think* it is?"

That was the last thing that ever came out of Kevin's mouth. I watched from the kitchen as Sid wrapped an arm around his neck blocking his airway. Kevin was immediately incapacitated. No longer in control of his own body, his face distorted and began to turn purple as he struggled against the grip. Sidney started to shake him violently, lifting his whole body up into the air and crashing him down on the tile until Kevin stopped struggling. The look on Sid's face was one of desperation. His lips parted and his own face reddened. As Sid's hold forced Kevin to the floor, still squeezing, I saw in him a sense of relief as a final jerk gave way to a sickening snap.

He quickly got to his feet and dragged the lifeless Kevin to the basement. I stood frozen, still in the entranceway to the kitchen when Sid reemerged.

"We need to get this done *now*, Sara," he explained in no uncertain terms. "We need to finish this."

A sense of urgency propelled me into action. My baby, safe with Caroline and waiting for us at the back sliding doors, remained a secret to the others. Since their return to the house, they had sequestered themselves in Skylab. Thoughts of Seth, and of their callous brutality, spurred me on. I was weak from the delivery, but strong enough to finish what I'd started.

As Sid and I met in the walk-out basement, we tossed what remained in our gas cans on the carpet that adorned the floor next to the fireplace.

"This is it," he said.

"This is it," I repeated, and lit the match.

Caroline handed my baby to me and the three of us stood back to watch the basement catch fire. The flames roared in my ears as they licked the ceiling, the heat intolerable within seconds.

"You go to safety now, Sara. You too, Caroline." Sidney's face had taken on a orange glow as he watched the fire dance through the house. "I'll watch that they don't get out."

Caroline looked worried, her forehead creased while her lips parted.

"No," I spoke up over the increasingly deafening sound of the flames. "I'll hide out in the field and wait for you both."

 Caroline smiled and touched the baby's head.

"We'll be right behind you, Sara."

"I know. Be safe, and see you soon." I turned and ran as fast as I could with Leif clenched tightly to my body and didn't stop running until the sound of the fire was just out of earshot. I threw down my heavy back pack and cradled Leif in his makeshift swaddle which hung around my shoulder and midriff, securing him to my chest.

I gasped for air a moment and sat down hard on the field floor. Then I watched as the fire began to crawl up the exterior walls and consume the roof. How could anyone escape something like that? Yet I watched. Just to be sure.

Chapter Twenty

My baby at my breast, I stared as the house I'd called home for over a year burned with a brightness that blotted out the moon and stars. Where were Sid and Caroline? They were all I had left. They shouldn't have stayed behind. There I was all alone, but they had been positioned right next to the exit, so surely nothing could have gone wrong. The house burned like a beacon in the night beyond the muddy expanse of the cornfields, framed by the blackened forest to the southwest and the dirt road coming to a T along the east.

Gun shots! I knelt and shielded Leif with my body. I wasn't so far away that a stray bullet couldn't find me. The shots rang in my ears as they became more frequent. I hadn't considered a shoot out.

"Please, let them get away," I whispered to the night, wishing for Caroline and Sidney to find me. I couldn't do this alone.

An explosion burst from the back of the house. I could feel the heat of it, even at this distance. The ground vibrated under my knees. The gas tank. I could almost taste it. The smell forced my free hand up to cover my mouth and nose.

I could barely make out a silhouette moving toward me and my baby. Were they running? I took a chance and screamed over the roar of the explosions. "Caroline?!" No answer. "Sid?" Still no answer. Next I cursed myself for having called out at all. If this wasn't either Caroline or Sidney, I had just given myself up to the enemy. Remembering Joel's pistol in my bag, I retrieved it. I made myself as small as I could in the dirt, careful not to make a sound. My child was strangely quiet under his sheet. Panicked by Leif's stillness, I unwrapped his head and kissed his warm cheek. He buried his face into my hand. Where was the silhouette? I'd lost them. Oh Jesus, I thought to myself. I held my breath and listened. Perhaps I'd imagined it?

The roar of the fire increased as it consumed more and more of the house, drowning out any footsteps in the field. But still, I waited, and watched.

I waited there, in that spot and watched the flames burn themselves out, all the while hoping to see Caroline and Sidney. But as the dawn approached, I knew I had lost them as well. I was now completely alone.

Chapter Twenty-One

My baby slept in his wrap tight to my chest, waking up three times through the night to eat, then drifting back to sleep, oblivious to the horror I had just witnessed. He wasn't feeding effectively yet, but this night, at least, he slept a little. I did not sleep. I panned the landscape for movement. Nothing. No one. A steady line of smoke twisted up into the ever brightening morning sky from a central point in the rubble. I heard a snapping from inside the house, then a crunching that went on and on. A wall collapsed in on itself and took the majority of the house along with it. The crash was deafening.

As I bent to stretch my lower back, my eyes locked on last night's silhouette. He was lying on the ground face down, not twelve feet from where I'd spent the night.

"Jesus," I said aloud. Which one was it? Earl? Freddy? Too tall to be Earl.

"Freddy!" I exclaimed, sure it was Fred. He did not respond. Shrapnel protruded from his back. He must have staggered out of the inferno, having escaped the flames through a second floor window, then been taken down by debris from the explosion. A large piece of metal was pointing towards the sky. His hair was crusty, scorched. His pants had stuck to his legs at the back. I wasn't sure his face would be recognizable but I turned it towards me to confirm his identity. It was Fred, his expression forever etched with a look of agony.

"*Earl.*" I spoke with contempt. I hated what he'd become. The way he'd taken the reins the past few months, the way he'd talked his way into the broken hearts and minds of our friends. After Joel, Earl had seized his opportunity. Unfortunately many of my friends, *our* friends, had fallen under his spell. The idea of revenge was a powerful tool. Earl knew it, and he used it to his advantage.

Now I found myself without a home, without a friend. Alone.

The baby rustled and began to whimper. I lifted my shirt. He screamed as I tried to nurse him. Why was it this hard? Sometimes getting him to nurse was mentally exhausting. I didn't have the tools they showed in the text books: the breast pump, the bottles. I hated to think of my baby as a burden. He was everything to me. But the lack of sleep and the endless torturous sessions at my breast were almost enough to make me shut down.

I was utterly exhausted. My eyes caught the sunrise moving behind the smoke, rising from the wreckage. The smoke blurred the colors, making the morning seem more sultry.

I was afraid to approach the smoldering rubble to look for Sid and Caroline. How could I do this on my own? But I had to. As my mind raced, I cautiously approached the remains of the house.

That's when I spotted them lying on their backs behind the pool, on the decline that led into the woods. They were motionless. To my horror I confirmed my friend's fate.

"Caroline! Sid!" I choked. I caressed Caroline's face and hugged her lifeless body against mine with one arm, Leif in the other, shaking all the while. But there was no wishing them back. I laid her back down, next to Sid. I kissed their heads and closed their eyes. I took their hands and interlocked their fingers. When I stood to look at them one last time I broke down and cried recklessly. The baby cried with me and I made no effort to sooth him.

They'd been shot point blank. Was it Fred, in one last evil act before he collapsed in the field with a piece of hot shrapnel in his back? Maybe Earl escaped and found them, exacting his revenge. I spun around, eyeing the woods and the rubble. Imagine, if it was all for nothing? The possibility tortured me. If Fred had nearly gotten away, why not Earl?

I took a deep breath, removed the water bottles and bags of food from Caroline and Sid's supplies, whispered *I'm so sorry*, and returned to the field. My mind spun with pent-up shock and grief. Nothing made sense anymore. All I knew for sure was that Sonny was headed east, and I had to go north with precious few items packed away in my backpack and a baby slung around my torso.

Chapter Twenty-Two

N orth. It was the one direction we had dared not explore too deeply. When Earl, Sonny, and Fred had returned from their expedition, they had horrible accounts of what we would find if we ventured in this direction. It was a killing field. Vehicles scattered across the highway for miles. Bodies on top of bodies, as if they'd died climbing over one another.

Why was I going north? South wasn't an option: it was flattened by the initial blast and fires still raged along the horizon. East we'd already covered for miles and the west was just more of the same: burned out townships barely capable of sustaining life. The north was unexplored beyond the word of three friends, friends that had become enemies.

I was still very scared, but I had been given hope. I had been in contact, to some degree, with our angel. That same angel Connor had seen and Joel had spoken to, that had guided Jake's last act and who had showed Sidney his path in overtaking the flags. This angel of ours had actively addressed many of us over the course of the last year, but never me. I couldn't understand how a guardian angel could let it get so bad for us. It seemed a desperate attempt to feel some sort of optimism. So transparent.

I was convinced that this angel concept had driven Joel mad. That and his addiction to the marijuana we'd pilfered that first week from the barn garden. Over time the stress of leadership, the angst he felt over the angel's plans concerning his destiny, and the constant smoking overwhelmed him. Then, when Connor was executed in front of us by Gareth, Joel had snapped completely, and to some degree I had blamed this angel of his for having ever causing Joel such hopelessness and despair. But when he finally spoke to me, I listened. It was an out. And so, I marched north.

Before I had ventured far, I felt something guiding me. Maybe it was just intuition. Or maybe Joel's angel was finally giving me some kind of hope to move forward on. Never before had I needed hope more. Even upon discovering the death of my entire family. Even upon learning that the world as we knew it had ceased to exist. Now, alone, with a baby strapped to my chest, I needed hope more than ever. So I listened. And something told me Joel was right. I should go north.

I continued, through my fatigue and fear. Travelling on foot with a new baby was going to prove difficult. If he wasn't crying, he was attempting to sleep or feed. The rumors I'd heard that breastfeeding was a cruel endeavor - something I'd picked up during a stint in the maternity ward during my final month of co-op – were true. But Leif had no other option, so we persevered. Sometimes it felt endless. He would cry for an hour, feed for ten minutes, then an hour later start all over again.

Leif had not 'attached' to my breasts like I had expected. Every other animal on the planet seemed to effortlessly attach to their respective mother's nipples, but human babies required weeks of practice and a team of nurses. What if *this* was the beginning of the end? What if nobody's babies would suckle anymore without these expansive support structures? I don't think Leif had had a satisfying feeding since he'd been born. Mostly he would fall asleep exhausted, never full. But looking at his face, so tiny, so helpless, gave me strength. I would live for him. I would do whatever I had to, to protect him.

*****

The days relinquished their light to the evenings as the sun was selfishly swallowed by the horizon. A gathering of storm clouds overhead. That night I settled down in a field as I had the night before, a single tree whose canopy of leaves had disappeared long ago offering little cover.

As I took a closer survey of our surroundings I saw a light flickering in the distance to the east. "Is that a house?" I wondered aloud.

It looked like candle light. But how far away was it? My perception of distance had all but left me. The monotonous flatness of the landscape and the colors, still mostly variations of grey, removed much of my ability to actually decipher one mile from ten. With so much of the forests burned to the ground and the old cattle and corn fields empty, the openness of everything left a person feeling very vulnerable. Turning back, I watched the clouds mirror the rest of the landscape – shades of grey. Up from down seemed a difficult separation.

I decided to move toward the light. A rusted cattle fence once employed to keep the cows and sheep from entering the adjacent corn field stood as a barrier between us and that light. I ran my hand across the brittle wire, careful not to take a sliver. The fence stood five feet high, just four or five inches shorter than me.

"We have to climb it, Leif," I told him. Our only other option was to follow the fence south until we hit the road again, but there was no time before the darkness made it impossible to navigate. I rubbed his back, his body wrapped closely to mine.

Who might that light belong to? What if it were a group of men? What if they hadn't seen a woman in months? I had my pistol, Joel's gun. And I had a few rounds of ammunition to go with it. I'd shied away from killing in the past, but I resolved myself to do whatever I had to do to protect my baby.

I threw my jacket on top of the fence. Climbing up was easy enough - it was navigating my legs over the top that proved difficult. The fence began to wiggle violently under my weight as my right leg shifted to the other side. "Shit, shit, shit…"

The top wire snapped as I attempted to lift my left leg. I tumbled to the wet earth with a thud, narrowly avoiding crushing Leif. He began to wail. Picking myself up, I pulled him out of his swaddle and kissed his cheeks, bouncing him for a time in my arms until he settled. He was hungry; so was I.

Suddenly there was a voice above me.

"Come child." It was a woman's voice. How was I caught so off guard? How did this woman know I was here? The crying. Still, where the hell did she come from?

"Quickly, the rains are coming." She took my arm and led me toward the flickering light. I followed, slowly relaxing.

It took all of one minute to reach a veranda in the middle of what might have been a yard in *life*. The remains of a house stood just a few meters away, mostly burned out, uninhabitable. The woman picked up the flickering gas lamp and raised it to my face. This was the light I had seen, the light I'd been drawn to like a moth.

"Come." She bent down and lifted a trapdoor in the center of the veranda. "We'll take you in." The old woman gestured that I walk down a ladder affixed to a dirt wall. With little other option, and a sense that this woman was genuinely trying to help us, I carefully navigated the darkness, feeling my way down each rung until I hit solid ground.

Turning, I saw more gas lamps, leading down a long corridor. Behind me, the old woman handed me her lamp and took the lead. "Follow me."

Chapter Twenty-Three

We were in a large room. This was a bomb shelter of some kind. To my left was a massive basin. Like the fuel tank at Joel's house. The ceiling was some twenty feet overhead and lined with cables and piping. The room itself was quite cozy: a smokeless fire burned in the far corner while rugs and furs seemed to cover the place from floor to ceiling. The lighting was dim, but my eyes rapidly adjusted to take it all in. The air was dry, and smelled of steel and leather.

"What is this place?" I asked.

"This is my home," the woman answered. "*Our* home," she corrected herself, panning an outstretched arm across the wall to my right. Here three other women sat staring at me. Each seemed to be performing some task; one knitting, another chewing at something, while the third rubbed a stone against a hide of some kind.

"Hello," I said meekly. Despite my fatigue and bewilderment, I was impressed. This was a well structured hideout. Had these four women survived all this time underground? "I'm Sara," I continued. "This is Leif." I rubbed my hand in a circular motion on the baby still wrapped across my chest.

The women nodded at me. I turned back to the old lady who brought me to the hideout. She was placing the lamp on a table, which was stacked high with dried, prepackaged fruit. "Have a mango, dear."

I was still wary, having learned most things were not what they seemed. Still, the fruit proved too much to resist. Eating the dried fruit, I felt a surge of energy.

"Your baby," said my hostess. "He is how old?"

"Just two days."

"Just two days," she repeated. She looked past me. "The child is two days old." The others nodded.

"Two days is right," said another one; I could see now that she was chewing the end of a rope. Bizarre.

This back and forth puzzled me, and since my baby was the topic of discussion, I fought down suspicion and worry.

"He is a Gemini." Another of the three women at the wall spoke up. "The messenger God rules his house from Mercury." She set her rock down and stared straight at me. "Instill a sense of *destiny* in Leif, and he will be that which he is meant to be."

The suggestion that Leif had a destiny upset me. Talk of destiny was all Joel ever spoke of in his sleep towards the end. To these women, Leif should only have been a baby. My brow raised and creased. My hostess read my face, but ventured another question.

"Where was Leif born, Sara?"

"Just an eight hour walk from here, to the south."

"It is as it should be then," said the last of the three women at the wall. "As you predicted."

"As Tages predicted," corrected my hostess.

"*He is great,*" the three said in unison.

This was becoming alarming. Was this a cult of sorts? Were they lulling me into a false sense of security so they could take my baby from me? My jaw flexed.

"We ask, Sara, because we need to be sure." The old woman rested a hand on my shoulder.

"Sure of what?"

"We've *seen,*" said the woman chewing the rope, her eyes narrowed to slits.

"What is it you think you've *seen?*" I crossed my arms over Leif, shielding him from what I feared might come.

"Tages has shown us."

"Who is *Tages?*"

"Tages is a divine being, with the appearance of a child, but the wisdom of an old man," explained my hostess as she circled round the table. "Tages is the ancient seer from the Etruscan religion."

"The Etruscan religion?" I did not relax my guard.

"It is an ancient religion which foretold everything that would ever come to pass."

"And my *son* is mentioned?"

"In not so many words, yes."

"How can you say that?"

"As we saw this end, we have seen a future end." The old woman at the table picked up a long wooden stick, a staff.

"Your religion predicted this end? *The Reaper?*"

"It predicted the outcome of the Reaper's threats, and is what drove us underground."

"You were prepared."

"We were." The woman chewing the rope appeared at my side suddenly. I jumped.

"Jesus Christ!" I shouted. Leif jolted, cried out. I pulled the sling over my head and set him on the table, all the while frowning at the thin woman. I turned him over and rubbed his back. He began to settle down.

"Tell me what you know," I demanded.

"Your child is guarded," the hostess explained, her head tilting sideways as she inspected him.

She picked him up and pulled him close to her emaciated face. Sunken eyes darted back and forth as she examined Leif. She blew along the silhouette of his head. I grimaced. What must this woman's breath smell of – *eyes of newt and wing of bat?* She studied him with an intensity that made me uncomfortable. Why had I handed my son over to this woman? Admittedly I had felt immediately drawn to her. But I could not be too trusting.

"He is guarded by the *others*. He has an *old* soul."

I shook my head and retrieved him. "What are you saying?"

"Your son's aura is like *fire*." She looked as though she had come out of a daze.

"So, what should that mean to me?"

"That means that he is a person of interest to the *other side*."

The *other side, the angel*, the undertones of what she was explaining made me want to scream. I became visibly shaken.

"Your aura spoke to me the moment I saw you," she said quietly. "I know you are confused, frustrated, angry, and so very sad. You have lost much, but no more than everyone else. It is what you have *gained* that is important now."

She understood so much about me, that I lowered my guard slightly. "Then what is it about us? Why has the *other side* shown such an interest in me?"

"Everything is for a reason."

"You wouldn't be so sure if you heard my story."

"Everything," she repeated. "We play off one another." She circled the table again. "It's like Shakespeare wrote: '*All the world's a stage, And all the men and women merely players; They have their exits and their entrances, And one man in his time plays many parts…*'"

"What is it you believe then? Is it fate, destiny?"

"I *believe*; that is enough."

"Do you believe everything that will ever be has already been determined?" I still had a hard time buying this theory. How could any sort of God or higher power have orchestrated the destruction of all it had created?

"There are many different paths, but ultimately, only one can play itself out. For that, we are *all* responsible."

"So choice - free will, that exists?"

"Yes, of course, this would all be little more than a dress rehearsal otherwise. For every path a script will be followed, but the path is a choice made by us all."

"What choice did we all have in the Reaper's decision?" I asked, challenging the old woman's theories.

"I only speak the wisdom of the Etruscans. That the path is written is how seers have seen. That is how *I* am able to see."

"You see the future?"

"Not in so many words. Destiny reveals itself to me through my practices. The Etruscans believed that among us exists an immutable course of divine will. They were devoted to the question and interpretation of destiny."

"Are you a psychic?"

"No. I admit, I am able to see auras, which is the energy emitted from an individual, but my abilities to read events and chart people's destinies are granted through the ancient practices passed down by the Etruscans."

"*Who* are the Etruscans?"

"An ancient people that were conquered and integrated into the Roman empire over two thousand years ago. They were wise in their ability to read the signs in nature by asking questions to Tages, their profit seer."

"How does it work?"

"You are curious, Sara. That's good; we have much to teach you." She lifted her stick and continued. "I use my staff to draw out an invisible frame to the sky and horizon." Her staff was a twisted branch maybe five feet in length and very thin. "Then I ask a question. The answer is interpreted in nature's reaction. It is a complex science. Perhaps more of an art."

My initial interest in this complete stranger's religion had grown into something more. What if she could tell me what would happen next? What if she could guide me and my son to safety? As crazy as it all sounded, the last year of my life demanded I approach this woman with an open mind.

"How can you be so sure it works?"

"I have seen it work, Sara. I have counseled dozens of people in my life through these means. When the Grimm Reaper was first mentioned in the news I drew my box and I watched the sky. I asked the question; *What might this threat bring about to the world?'* Within two minutes I had my answer. A raven flew into my magical field, and upon entering it dropped out of the sky. Dead."

My skin crawled; was it the story or the story teller? Either way, this woman both unsettled and reassured me. What if she could help me make sense of this chaos?

"The dead bird was nature's answer..." I trailed off.

"Yes, an obvious interpretation of what would come to pass."

"And so did you try to stop it?"

"As powerful as one person's actions can be, I knew that any warning on my part would fall on deaf ears. The powers that be would not succumb to the Reaper's demands. We *all* knew that. And when five billion people share a common idea, it is impossible to change that path."

"So you holed up in here? Waiting?"

"I did. I waited, I prepared. I told only those I thought could help."

A sense of destiny suddenly overcame me, not for myself so much as for my son.

"I invite you to stay here, until we have your baby healthy and strong. His destiny will be realized to you in time, and in between that time and now there is here. "

The offer to stay was very appealing. I was lucky to have crossed their path, I knew that. She obviously noticed Leif's small size and weakened state. She understood I had been having trouble latching him to my nipple. "Yes," I said. "Yes, I would very much appreciate that. Staying I mean. You're kind to take us in."

"Of course we would, Sara."

"I-I need to feed him. Have you any milk?"

"He's having difficulties at your breast."

"Yes. He'll eventually latch on, but not without a fight, and even then, it's not much."

"We will help you." She opened a cupboard and revealed several tins of powdered baby formula. She turned to see the surprised look on my face. "We have prepared for your arrival."

Chapter Twenty-Four

The women were living in a cold war bomb shelter built by my hostess' father in the Sixties. Her name was Bethany. She was a pale and wrinkled woman who'd spent her whole life in her father's house. When he died twenty years before, she'd taken over the household, and with no brothers or sisters, no husband and a mother incapable of looking after herself, there she remained. Her father had revealed the underground structure to her when she was just a little girl. She had never been allowed to enter the space while he was alive. When she had returned home from his funeral, she finally entered it for the first time. There she found a stash of forty year old food tins and provisions long forgotten since the threat of nuclear war had vanished from conscious awareness.

But after having read the future promised to the world with her magic, she had the bomb shelter retro-fitted. That happened just one year before the end came. The smokeless fireplace, the kitchen, toilets and dry storage, all of it was improved and expanded upon. Bethany had spent her life savings on the project: she was so certain of our end.

The storage of food looked barely touched though the four women had lived in the shelter since before the bombs fell. As I became more at home with the women, I found chores to do to earn my keep. Leif had become quite a bit chubbier after only a week underground. The fact that Beth had a massive supply of baby formula convinced me of her ability to see the future.

"It wasn't so much that I *saw* the future, or that I saw you and little Leif showing up at my door," Beth explained as she shook another bottle of the milk and handed it to me. "I did, however, see the baby."

"How do you mean?" I asked.

"Like I said, I can see a person's aura. Yours is quite beautiful by the way, Sara. Bluish orange." I blushed. "But your son's…." She chuckled ironically. "Your son's aura is a *fire.* You might say I saw his *aura.* One night, as I pondered the concept of the Yin and Yang, I realized that if someone were to plunge the world into despair, another would rise to pull us out. So, I drew my magic frame on the horizon, first to the north, then the west, the east and finally the south asking the same question, *From where will our savior approach?* Then a great light shimmered in my magical envelope and I knew – I knew the direction you'd come to find us. I knew it would be an aura I would see. I suspect his father's aura would have been quite something to see as well."

"He was the leader of our group."

"Yes, I imagine he was. He must have been a good boy. You are a good girl, Sara, and Leif will command the respect of men as his father did, with compassion and with love."

"Yes," I trailed off a moment, remembering Joel. "He was a very kind man. It's just…"

"Never mind what has been." She waved her hands wildly. "Leif is here now. He is yours and his father's prodigy. You are his rock. Speak only highly of his father and remember that *you* are his teacher, his guardian, his everything."

Leif pushed his stomach out, arching his back as he sucked at the bottle, moving against my arm. I smiled down at him, my heart filled with a love I hadn't imagined.

"It was Leif's aura I saw." She panned the south-west wall with her outstretched arm. "Coming from the direction you said you'd come from, the same day you said he'd been born. His aura was like a light haze on the horizon, where no such light had occurred prior to putting the question to Tages."

Beth walked to her bed, which was positioned alongside the others. She sat at the edge and removed her shoes. "Tages is great," she said, and laid down to sleep.

"Thank you so much for taking us in." Tears welled up in my eyes.

"You are very welcome dear. You are a messenger of hope, in a time of great sorrow."

Chapter Twenty-Five

Occasionally we would venture outside. Jenny, the woman who read horoscopes, insisted that the baby spend quality time outdoors, when the sun was out. Jenny was a heavier woman; I thought it quite likely she was morbidly obese in *life* the way the skin hung from her neck and arms. Her face was kind, with not many lines for her age, which she said was sixty-seven. She, Leif and I would take walks around the burnt frame that once housed Bethany and her parents.

"It must have been a beautiful home," I commented.

"It was in Beth's family for generations. They were farmers. Beth made the decision to burn the house in an effort to keep would-be squatters and groups seeking shelter a comfortable distance away from our hiding place."

"Smart. And you? Did you live nearby?"

"No, I lived in the city. Beth and I knew each other from the Expo circuit, Beth offering her aura readings and predictions and me with my horoscopes." She shifted her heavy rifle from one shoulder to the other.

"Do you still read horoscopes?"

"I have read your son's according to my star charts and am currently putting it together. We can discuss it another time."

"I'd love that." Completing our umpteenth circle we headed back into the tunnel as the sun set in the west.

*****

We spent our time listening to music, baking, cleaning, maintaining equipment and appliances, and entertaining Leif. I felt very safe underground. The seals on the shafts that opened up to the rest of the world were military grade. They locked like a submarine, virtually airtight. Air was circulated through grates that could pass as sewer covers to anyone the least bit interested, but they could never open them. It seemed the perfect hiding place from the world at large.

Leif was gaining weight at a surprising rate after two weeks with an unlimited supply of food. The women were very understanding over his quirks and late night feedings. They helped when I asked and offered when I didn't. It was like having four midwives at my service 24/7. I wouldn't have had it this good in *life*. My thoughts often turned to my own parents when I looked at Leif. They would have been so proud, perhaps not that their 19-year old daughter had given birth before entering college, but that they were grandparents. I tried not to think too much about my family. All that accomplished was to make me angry, and sad, and I needed to stay as happy as possible for Leif's sake.

Sally was another of the four women sharing her space with Leif and I. She was around forty years old and very thin, even more so than Beth. I worried for her. She never seemed to be eating, and when I thought I saw her chewing it was on that damn rope of hers.

"It keeps me from overeating," she would tell me.

I would fight her on her logic. "You barely eat as it is, Sally. There's not much left of you."

"Never mind Sally," Beth would say. "She's a vain one! Waiting on her Prince Charming to arrive and take her away from all of this."

"It could happen!" she shouted.

"How many times do you need to shuffle that deck of yours before you believe that it isn't?" Sally was a Tarot card reader and, as I found out, also a friend from the Expo circuit.

"What sort of Expos did you ladies attend exactly?" The question had been on my mind since Jenny had mentioned it.

"Psychic fairs, and things of that nature," Jenny piped in while busily loading the ten disc CD player. "Sally was a whiz with those cards. You should let her read your cards, Sara."

"Actually, Tarot cards scare me. Like Ouija boards. I've always steered clear of them. No offence, Sally."

"None taken. I dislike the Ouija board too. *Evil* contraption!" I noted a sarcastic tone in her voice.

"I think we can all agree the Ouija board is a powerful portal that should only be handled by a professional." Beth had a playful look on her face.

"A *professional?*" I asked. "What do you call a professional Ouija board user?"

"A medium." Carol spoke up from her corner. She rarely spoke at all, never mind to me. She slipped out of her dark corner where she spent most of her time reading and re-reading a giant volume of some kind. She kept a comfortable chair, a side table and lamp that looked as though it were pilfered from a Psychic expo. She was the creepy one of the four.

"The Ouija *is* a portal, and yes, it should only be accessed by a medium. Someone with a higher understanding of what you're letting into the waking world." As she moved past me, her long black hair brushed my face and smelled of olive oil.

"I used one once, with my friends when we were fourteen," I said. "There were four of us: two boys and two girls. My friend said we should pair up, boy-girl because it worked better that way."

"True," Carol confirmed. She sat next to me at the table, running her olive-skinned fingers through her long black hair.

"Yeah, so we did," I continued. "It was crazy what happened. We asked questions about silly things mostly but then my friend, Julia, asked something of the spirit."

"And what did she ask?" Carol stared through me, anticipating my answer.

"Well, I remember its name was Samuel, the *spirit* or whatever it was."

"Spirit. That is your best case scenario."

"I guess." I was pleased that Carol was so interested in my story. "Anyways, Julia asked it to prove its presence to us."

"And did it?"

"Yes. The lights went off a moment after she'd challenged it, and we ran out of the basement screaming."

"Your friend conjured a powerful spirit." She looked reproachfully at me. "And so you never played with it again?"

"No." I felt a chill run through me. "That scared me half to death."

"Breaking the connection like that can sometimes leave the spirit in our plane. I wonder if your friend ever suffered a similar experience in her basement again."

My eyes popped and my head involuntarily cocked back. "She did actually. Many times after that night, whenever she went into the basement the light would turn off. She found an excuse to never go back down there. And she never did."

Carol stood and put on the kettle. "It's not a safe game to play. Spirits can become very resentful when left to linger in our plane, and depending on the spirit, or *demon*, they can become a poltergeist."

"Why do they sell that game to children?"

"I wish they never had. There are countless souls that have been left behind in our world, condemned to isolation as a result of the Ouija. As a medium, I used to cleanse homes of spirits, showing them the light. Many of them manifested from the Ouija."

"That's so sad. If I'd known we were hurting anyone…."

"That's the trouble with the Ouija board: they made it a *game*, and so the majority take it as a sleight-of-hand from a friend when they first experience anything." She pulled her long black hair back into a ponytail and tied it. "It is almost *never* a sleight-of-hand."

Bethany attempted to lighten the mood. "Okay Carol, don't scare the poor girl. She's innocent."

"*Ignorant* is more apt a description, but I understand your point. It's just that I *feel* their sadness, the spirits, when I cleanse a house. Lucky for your friend it was not a demon that answered your call. A demon can follow you for the rest of your life. It can interfere with your life in ways you cannot know."

I went white at that. Julia had never really been the same after the experience: Christ, she'd *killed* herself eventually. What if her spirit was a demon that finally took its vengeance? I shook the thought from my head. No, it was the circumstances that forced her hand, not a *demon*.

"Carol summons spirits even now," Jenny called over from the couch. "She confers with them on things that may come to pass. She is one of the reasons we were prepared for you. In fact, after Bethany came to us with her vision of Leif's impending aura, we all used our crafts to pinpoint the time and place of his arrival."

"A wonderful coincidence that he was born an eight hour walk from here," I teased.

"Well, we could go into coincidences with you, Sara, but I think for right now you've heard enough of spirits, demons, auras and the like." Bethany poured the boiled water into a tea pot and placed it on the table.

"No, I am very interested," I assured them. "I have always been a spiritual person. The Bible is something I'd always held very close to my heart."

"The Bible you say?" Sally moved her tiny frame to the table and took her seat. "There's a book I have not picked up in a long time."

"I had written it off myself a few months ago, after our friend Connor was taken from us. But I've revisited it since. Better to have faith in something than none at all."

"Faith, hope, belief, they are what they are." Sally picked up her cup. "The thing about faith is that it comes from within rather than from without. If you get my meaning."

"That it exists at all at a time like this is enough, I should think," Jenny offered. "That is enough for me, for now."

"We had *faith* Leif would come." Bethany sat too, and poured herself a cup of the hot tea. "You are an example of our faith, in our abilities to *see*." She tipped her cup at me.

Leif began to fuss and cry, so I got up from the table and moved to the couch. The others sat drinking their tea, quietly. "You're a *vision*, Leif," I whispered at him, smiling. I bounced him on my knee until he calmed down.

"Take what we tell you to heart, Sara," Sally called from the table, her back to me. The others turned to look at me and I nodded appreciatively at them. They were a coven of witches. What did they call that? A Wiccan? I knew there was no mistake that I had found my way here. They were too sure of themselves, too confident. I mean, why else would you stock baby formula?

*****

My Tarot card reading commenced the following evening. Sally sat across from me at the kitchen table. Her thin fingers shuffled a deck of cards much larger than what I was used to. She placed them in front of me and asked me to cut them.

"This isn't like poker is it? 'Cut the deck, cut your throat?'" I asked playfully.

"No," she replied.

"Okay." I cut the deck.

She explained that she used a very old Tarot card spread with its roots in 16th-century France. She would place seven cards on the table in a circle, with an eighth in the center representing the planets.

"Does it count that Pluto isn't considered a planet anymore?"

"No."

"Okay, what next?"

"Now ask your question. What would you like to know?"

"I think I should ask about Leif. What will he be like as a man, what is his destiny? Will that work or does it have to be about me?"

"No, it can be about anyone. Is that your question then? What is Leif's destiny?"

"Yes, that's my question."

"Very well." She smiled and began placing the cards in order. "If the card is upside down, the meaning changes. Each card placement represents a planet and the planets rule different aspects of our lives."

"Okay." I was excited to get a sneak peek into Leif's adulthood. Tarot scared me only because my mother had been frightened off by a Tarot reader she'd visited once. She told me the reader had only negative things to say and that he even went as far as to tell her when she would die and how! I swore I'd never do this, but in light of what these women were capable of, I felt at least curious to learn what I could about Leif's future.

Sally flipped the first card. "This is his Earth card. It represents the here and now. He has pulled an inverted *8 of Cups* card. Someone close to him will abandon Leif in a time of great urgency. He will feel betrayed at the moment, but perhaps realize that this person's personal quest was necessary for their own growth, and his."

I frowned.

The second card was the *9 of Cups*, also inverted. "This is the Moon card, relating to those things immediately surrounding or affecting the subject. Leif will find he is either seen as someone who is a false prophet, exuding a false display of power or promise to those that surround him, or he will recognize another as such."

"Ha!" she exclaimed as she turned the next card. "This is the Mars card, representing those issues in adversity to Leif, opposing his position. You see he's pulled the *7 of Wands* card, *courage*. Courage, to seize the day. To act decisively in the face of opposition. He will find himself standing up against injustice, taking an aggressive posture against his foe."

"That sounds like our Leif," called Bethany from the couch. I smiled at her.

"The next card is his Jupiter card, representing achievement, gain and expansion." She carefully turned the card to reveal a frightening sight. The Devil! Sally looked up at me sensing my disappointment.

"This is not a *bad* card, Sara. It may look intimidating, but it has many meanings. And look at that. It too is inverted."

"Okay, so what does this represent?"

"The inverted devil card represents an exercise in self-control. An act of selflessness, to avoid distraction and maintain one's sights on their path ahead. Leif will likely and selflessly throw himself onto the proverbial fire at some stage in his adult life, as he works towards what end he has in sight. This act will propel him into the leadership role he is destined to achieve."

She moved on to the fifth card in the pattern. "The ringed planet Saturn represents judgment and an overall assessment of Leif's position." She flipped it quickly. "Ah!" She looked back at her friends seated on their couch. "An inverted *7 of Cups*."

"This is a good card?"

"This represents a desire reborn. A job completed. An overriding will to fulfill what was started. Essentially, hard work bears great fruits." Her smile faded as she continued reading the card. "Leif will have realized his efforts but lose someone very close to him. You see in the card the undetermined figure walking off with a cup? This person means very much to Leif, but they will have abandoned him, either for their own selfish pursuits or for reasons of a spiritual nature. Regardless, Leif will feel very alone in his victory."

"That's sad."

"Yes, but it's the bigger picture that matters and your son knows this."

She turned the sixth card. "Mercury traditionally gives insight into business and professional matters, business associates or acquaintances. He has pulled the *4 of Cups*. This card offers clarity of thought in its inverted manifestation. Leif will see a clear path ahead, knowing what he wants for himself and humanity. His ability to meditate will have reached its summit."

The seventh card was turned. "Venus," she said. "You know what Venus is all about. Love, relationships. It is right side up." She smiled from ear to ear. "Our Leif will find his bliss in a relationship. He will also find he is surrounded by positive energies and an abundance of generosity. Good friendships and a sharing of good times evolve from his efforts. He is happy, happier than he has ever been."

Tears welled up and I wiped them away. "Sorry," I said, sniffling. "I'm just so happy to hear he'll be alright, that he'll fall in love."

"It could also act as a card of memories - items that have been in a person's life but have vanished. Leif may look to the elements in his childhood to solve problems in later life situations. Perhaps a return to innocence is his bliss. A relationship can be a physical thing, but it can also be spiritual."

"The Sun." The last card pulled, in the center of the circle, represented aspirations, fame and accomplishments. "Leif has pulled the *Justice* card."

Sally let out a great sigh of relief. "And it is right side up." She turned again to her friends at the wall and gave a nod. They nodded back at us.

"This is good also?"

"Look at the illustration on the card, Sara. The scales represent perfect equilibrium. The sword represents being able to cut to the heart of a matter quickly and keenly. The scales are also the balance of present and future. This tells us Leif has taken responsibility for his actions, realizing that everything he'd done in the past had shaped him, and everything that he'll do in the future would continue to do so. Leif will have reaped what he had sown. Much of the future depends upon what he's done in the past. Leif will have reached a perfect balance."

I was overwhelmed by all of this information. I wasn't sure what to make of it. That the reading had been mostly positive made me happy. I was beginning to really trust these women and their *feelings*. But just as with the *angel* Joel and some of the others claimed to have seen, part of me would always be skeptical.

"This is a good reading." Carol stood and moved through the room towards where Leif lay nestled on my lap, oblivious to all of the energy being generated in determining his future. "I would like to perform a séance with the boy. There is a great deal of spiritual energy surrounding him. The *others* are busy."

"What would a séance do?" I was nervous about this next step into the unknown. A séance was like the Ouija board to me, a dark, misunderstood magic of sorts, talking to the dead and all that.

"I will be better able to speak with the boy's guides, to know what they know."

"I don't know…"

"It's up to you of course, Sara, but it is in the boy's best interest that I perform a séance. The more we know, the more guidance we can offer you."

"Okay, if you truly believe it's in Leif's best interest, I'll consider it."

"Enough for tonight," Beth interrupted. "We have enough now to meditate on. Give the girl time to decide." With that the women retreated to their cots.

*****

The two days following Leif's Tarot reading gave me plenty to think about. Leif's life plan was beginning to take shape and with it, mine. As I rummaged through the cold room, another fifteen steps below the bunker, Carol approached me.

"Have you made a decision as to whether you'd like for me to speak to Leif's guide?"

"I think so."

"Good, Sara. Good. I have a strong feeling this guide can help you."

"How can you know that?"

"My own guide has warned me against channeling this spirit."

"Then maybe you shouldn't, Carol."

"Perhaps." She tilted her head to the left and looked down timidly. "But it is *because* of my guide's warning that I feel I must try."

"If you're sure."

She smiled and nodded. "I'll prepare for the séance. After dinner, we'll begin."

Chapter Twenty-Six

The bunker was usually quite dark, but the night of the séance only candle light was permitted, making the intimate space feel slightly more claustrophobic. We huddled around the circular kitchen table, hands joined. Leif had been put to bed and could be heard soundly snoring from his bassinette. Of course the women had furnished a portion of the bunker with baby furniture in anticipation of Leif's arrival.

I sat between Carol and Jenny. Their hands were vastly different: Jenny's pudgy and soft, while Carol's were bony and strong, but both were ice cold.

"We will begin by clearing our minds. Then focus on me. I will require your energies if I am to pull this off." Sally took a deep breath, held it for what seemed like ten seconds and slowly released it over another ten seconds. The others followed suit and I too took a deep breath, held it and released.

"Good, I can feel your energies entering my space," she whispered. "Now focus on Leif, focus on his *spirit*."

I thought of my son and smiled; he was snoring so loudly. My chest filled up with love and I almost laughed out loud. Carol's grip tightened and I squeezed back. Suddenly, Carol's head tilted back and her eye lids fluttered violently. I turned to Bethany and mouthed: "Is she alright?"

Beth nodded back.

"Concentrate." Carol pronounced each syllable. "I *see* him. It's a *him*." Her brow furrowed. "He is…. *dark*."

That gave me goose bumps. *He is dark?* I didn't like the sound of that.

"He's here now," she whispered. Her eyes shot open. "He's with Leif."

My head swung around to watch the crib. Nothing.

"I will try to make contact." The room fell silent. Everyone closed their eyes but me. I kept both on Leif.

"He's very powerful," Carol said through clenched teeth. "He's showing me he is in control. Our light does not attract him." She became suddenly rigid. "Speak to me," she pleaded. "Speak to me. Why do you attach yourself to this child?"

Silence.

"Tell me what you know of Leif's path so that we might help guide him." More silence.

"Yes... yes, I am listening..." Without opening her eyes, she began to relate the spirit's message.

"He says everything is as it should be." Her eyebrows met in the middle and her head shook back and forth. "He feels guilt over something. He is *sad*. He carries a deep emotional burden. He won't share what it is with me. He assures me his is a special task and that everything is as it should be."

She broke the circle by freeing hands, and looked at me. "He's a shadow, this spirit. He's like a silhouette. I can't really *see* him; he's blocking me. I can do no more." She took a deep breath. "I wish I could have helped him. He suffers a terrible guilt."

"You did well, Carol." Sally smiled at her.

"You can only help those that want to be helped, Carol," said Jenny. "You know that."

"I know." Carol wiped away a tear.

"So Leif is in good company with this spirit?" My concern was for my son and not the spirit that was apparently haunting him.

"He is a good spirit, Sara, rest easy in knowing that. And *powerful*. Leif is in good company. The spirit's sadness should not affect his goal."

"And this spirit's goal is what? To guide Leif's life toward some future purpose?"

"Exactly. He is your son's spirit guide."

Chapter Twenty-Seven

My time at the bunker with these witches was one of the most educational and spiritual experiences of my short life. Some days we sat to sip tea, play board games, or read one of the hundreds of magazines and books Beth had collected in preparation for this period. But on other occasions, one of them would take me aside to teach me some sort of lesson. In one such case, it was Beth herself.

"Take this pendulum." She handed me a delicate chain necklace with a ring threaded through it. "Hold it like this." Taking my hand, she raised my arm up. When my hand was at eye level, she pulled the chain out of my fist slowly until the ring hung six inches from my fingers. "I'll show you what we're all capable of, not just me. What you see is not all that makes up the world we live in. Energy is all around us. *We* are energy and we *emit* energy. When you feel the body heat of another, do you not believe it comes from them?"

"Yes."

"But you cannot see it, can you?"

"No."

"You cannot see radio waves, or microwaves, but you know they exist because science can measure them. Science cannot measure what a psychic sees or how a healer heals. The only way to believe is to experience."

"Okay. Help me understand."

"We lost many of our abilities to technology. Our gifts were left unexplored. Now, in this new world, we must rely upon our natural gifts, our abilities to *see* and to heal."

"Teach me."

"Quiet your hand, child." She wrapped her wrinkled hands around my clenched fist. I stopped shaking. The pendulum went still. "Now with a thought make the pendulum swing."

"With a thought?"

"Yes. Concentrate on the ring and make it move. It is a powerful practice, a first step in your own realization that within you is a power far greater than anything you might have imagined."

I studied the ring and silently asked it to move. I thought about creating a whirlwind beneath it, twirling it counter-clockwise. It didn't take any time at all for the pendulum to actually move and then quicken. It was spinning around and around and I could barely believe it. Then it slowed to a stop. The smile that had grown on my face out of awe gave away my fascination with what had just occurred.

"Exciting, isn't it?"

I nodded. "But it stopped."

"Because you willed it to stop."

"I didn't."

"You did, by not quite believing what you were doing. You might have thought your fingers or your wrist were twitching just enough to make the pendulum swing, or you simply couldn't accept that what was happening was in fact happening. You lost faith."

"I was *really* doing that with my mind, with a thought?" My hand lowered and I rubbed my shoulder.

"You were. There is more I can show you. Lift your arm again and make the pendulum move back and forth in a straight line rather than in a circle."

I did as she asked. I concentrated again, and mentally saw the ring moving back and forth. Seconds later it actually did. The smile returned to my face.

"Good, good, Sara, you're doing very well. Now imagine the circular motion means *no*, and the back and forth *yes*."

"Okay." I focused on the ring.

"Now ask a question."

"And this will give me my answer?"

"If it is a yes or no question, you will have your answer."

Why not? I was intrigued. "Will my son be blond?"

The pendulum slowed and changed direction. It was whipping around in a circle.

"I guess not!" I grinned at Bethany.

I felt empowered. I kept asking questions and it kept answering. Right or wrong I couldn't say, but I hoped the future would confirm my hope that what I was learning wasn't all a hoax, and there really was something to what these women were teaching me.

Chapter Twenty-Eight

The following day it began to rain violently. Thunder could be heard rumbling and crashing overhead. This made a trip around the perimeter out of the question, so I relaxed on the comfortable couch with a book. Leif was sleeping soundly in his crib. Suddenly, Jenny approached with an excited smile on her face. "I've finished it."

"What, Jenny?"

"Leif's horoscope."

I had completely forgotten Jenny was working on an elaborate explanation of Leif's existence via her star charts.

I sat up, placing the book on the coffee table. "That's great!" I motioned for her to sit next to me. As she sat, the couch groaned in protest beneath her weight.

"I think this will give you a good understanding of who your son is."

"I'm very interested. You know, I used to always read my horoscope." I don't know if I always believed it, but some days it seemed pretty dead-on. Weird.

"Good, then you're familiar with the idea behind the art."

"I think I get it," I nodded, anxious to get started. Truth be told, I knew that people born of the same astrological signs were said to share similar personality traits and even physical traits. But my knowledge of this art was weak at best.

Jenny laid out several pieces of paper in front of me on the table and began.

"So, your son was born June 20th of this year. This puts him under the sign of Gemini in the Zodiac."

"Yep, he's a Gemini."

She nodded. "I mentioned he was ruled by Mercury, the messenger god of Roman mythology. I think it fitting he should be ruled by Mercury. Perhaps his is a message of hope." Jenny was so confident in her proclamations, it almost made me smile. But I contained my amusement. I knew these readings were her life's work.

"Gemini is the third sign of the Zodiac. Gemini, the twins, are a mix of the yin and yang and are *never* boring!" She smiled.

"According to my charts, I can tell you where Leif will fall into the very best and the very worst of the Gemini traits." She placed a chubby finger on top of a pile she stacked in front of me.

"Leif will be very capable of seeing both sides of every story. This will help him as a leader to understand conflict and make educated decisions as to a solution. He will make a very good politician, and I mean good in the sense that he would actually be fair, honorable, well-loved by those who know him." I glanced at my sleeping baby, trying to picture him in this light. He sighed heavily and raised an arm across his face, as if this were all too much for him.

"Leif will be a very social person. He will be interested in developing relationships with people. Again, a wonderful trait for a leader. The Gemini is very intellectually-minded, authentically concerned with gathering information from those around them and rationalizing everything. Leif will be exceptionally intelligent, taking this gift to new heights."

"It's fun being able to visualize Leif as a person!" I was truly enjoying this. It had been so long since I had been able to feel anything akin to hope for the future.

"I'm glad you're taking this to heart, Sara. You've been very eager to understand our crafts and I'm sure your curious nature will help feed Leif's characteristics every bit as much as his birth sign."

She moved the top page to the back and continued with her explanation.

"Because Leif is a Gemini he will be mutable. Mutable people are flexible. They can go with the flow, they are adaptable and dexterous, and they are capable of tackling many things at once. Your son will be very curious, as you are, Sara."

She slipped the next sheet under the pile and moved on.

"Leif is an air element. This addresses his ability to think through a problem by gathering information. This element is a thinking-person's sign.

"Leif will have to be careful not to become detached from his course. A Gemini can become easily bored once they have achieved a goal. If he is aware of this pitfall, he can be mindful to avert it.

"One last thing, Sara. Leif should encourage his ability to find people's weaknesses, especially where it concerns their character. This particular trait I see being a very useful tool in his life."

She neatly organized her stack of papers, pushing them into my hands. Apparently she was finished. The loosening skin on her enormous arms flapped happily as she brushed her hands, indicating the end of our session.

"Thank you. Thanks so much for doing this." I really appreciated all the attention these women paid to my son. If nothing else, they were selling me on his destiny.

Chapter Twenty-Nine

Two months into my stay with my witches, I witnessed a bizarre event that heralded both an ending and a new beginning.

It was early morning. I had been up for a half hour feeding Leif at my breast in my cot. It had been a long hard fight, but over the course of two months we had finally gotten Leif to latch on and now he wanted this attachment all the time.

A sound suddenly emanated from Bethany's bed, like a thick rumble from deep in her throat. It was unusual for anyone to be awake this early, so I turned and wrote it off as Beth clearing her throat. Then I heard a tumble of blankets to the floor. I shifted to get a better view and gasped. Beth was sitting upright in bed, eyes closed, mouthing something. She didn't appear to be awake at all, but a series of words were forming a sentence now, in a low repetitive drone. I strained to understand what she was saying. I leaned closer.

"Go north, go north, go north."

Standing, Leif still attached at my breast, I backed away and collided with the open shelves. Pots and pans fell loudly to the steel floor. This snapped Bethany out of her trance rather violently. She seemed stunned to have woken up in a seated position. The others had awoken too, their eyes turning to Beth, who was confused to say the least.

"What happened?" Carol sat up too.

"It was Beth. She was chanting in her sleep and it frightened me. I'm sorry to have woken you all." Leif was crying from the violent abruption to his feeding and I bounced him back and forth on my hip.

"What was she chanting?" Carol looked at me solemnly.

"I can't be sure. I think… I think she was telling me to go north."

Carol stared into my eyes, looking me up and down. "Sara, it is time."

"Time?" I questioned.

"Time to continue your journey towards Leif's great purpose."

I stared back at her, dumbfounded. I had no desire to leave the comfort of this bunker my son and I called a home. Were they telling me to leave?

"It's time to go," Beth said plaintively, staring at me.

"I-I don't want to *go*," I said indignantly. "I'm not leaving." Tears welled up in my eyes.

"It's not up to us, Sara. Leif's guide has spoken through Beth. It is time to go." Carol stood and walked to one of the closets and pulled out a large black bag that resembled a suitcase with wheels. "You can use this to carry your things, as well as water and food."

"I'm not leaving," I repeated. "No. I can't go out there with an infant." I couldn't believe this was happening.

"You knew this was coming, Sara." Bethany approached me, her hands extended.

"I don't want to leave." I started to cry. I couldn't help it; I was completely overwhelmed.

"This isn't a choice, Sara. We have been given a clear sign to keep you moving north. Trust us. If you delay, the order of things may be irrevocably changed. You cannot take this sign lightly."

"If we could keep you here we would, Sara. Believe that." Jenny's kind eyes fell on mine.

"It is not Leif's destiny to stay any longer," Sally reminded me.

With that, they began moving silently through the bunker, collecting items for my journey. I sat on the bed and wept. This was what life had become. A series of disappointments. All I could do was carry on, but had no idea how. Or where I would end up.

Chapter Thirty

The weather was agreeable. The sun was starting to burn away the clouds in the east, which told me the day would be hot.

"Go north," Beth said with conviction. "Your destiny lies there."

"Thank you for everything." My voice cracked. "We would have been lost without you."

"Your stay here has run its course. We only helped you help yourself." She lowered her staff and opened her arms. I hugged her hard, as I was prone to do with the people I loved, and I could truly say I had grown to love this woman.

"I'll never forget you," I said, pulling away from her.

"I don't ask that you remember me, Sara, only that you remember your destiny. Go now, march Leif towards *his* destiny."

The wind picked up, blowing my hair into my face. As I brushed it out of my eyes Bethany had disappeared, back down the ladder, back down her rabbit hole. I would never forget her, and I would be sure Leif never forgot either.

As I marched away from my former home, I began to walk with renewed purpose. It was almost autumn, one of my favorite times of year. In *life* I would have been bombarded with colors framing the farmer's fields, dancing across the dirt roads, carried through the air on a fall breeze. The air would smell of the encroaching cold, making a day like today- warm and sunny- a real treat for the senses. The fields would be bare save the wheat, bundled in tidy rolls, awaiting transport.

As I remembered autumns past, I inhaled deeply, hoping to reconnect with my youth. I had read somewhere that smell was a powerful memory trigger. If I could be transported, if only for a moment, to a time when life was simpler....

I coughed, waking the baby wrapped tightly to my chest. The air was missing the distinct scent of leaves, of soil, of life. It was dry, and burned my throat. Even now, months after the rains had returned with the sun, and the planet seemed to be returning to some semblance of its former self, it was still a foreign place with little more color than shades of grey. The sun was shining. The sky was a brilliant blue, but when would I see a bud on a tree? When would a blade of grass defy the odds and push through the dead soil? When would life really begin again?

I knelt at the side of the road and released Leif from his wrap. He cried and I missed the old women immediately. Back in our hideaway, they would have swarmed around us and rushed little Leif off to soothe him to sleep. But such loving intrusions were gone now. We were headed for a different place: our destiny.

When finally Leif settled down and slept, it was late morning, and I felt I had a lot of ground to cover. I didn't know what lay ahead. But I knew there was nothing here, not anymore. And to get to somewhere, anywhere, I felt I had a long way to go. I could only hope Leif and I would find a safe place to put our heads before the sun set. Jenny had mentioned a fairground with outbuildings not far from the bunker, within a day's travel, admitting she had spent too many months on the carnival circuit. I only hoped I was heading in the right direction.

*****

Hours later, as the sun dipped below the horizon of naked trees, spreading shadows like a thousand emaciated fingers reaching hundreds of feet across the barren fields, I was exhausted. My feet were already blistered in my worn sneakers, and my back ached from carrying Leif. It was fortunate then that I came across Jenny's fairground. But what remained left no impression of the carnivals of my youth. Instead, I was walking into a nightmare.

A déjà-vu overcame me and I shook it off violently. I hated those things, but took comfort in a comment Seth had made to Joel once. Something about déjà-vu acting as an indicator - a marker for your life, telling you that you're on the right path.

I hugged the gutters and then rushed across the four lane highway to the retaining wall in front of the main entrance. The wall stood about eight feet high and swung around the west side of the park in a long creeping curve that ascended another foot or two at its peak. If I climbed up the wall and scurried along the top, I could hop the fence at some point rather than take my chances by walking right through the front gates. I smiled in satisfaction when I found a portion of the fence that had been pushed in and now rested on the roof of one of the attractions. Was this a former secret entrance for teenagers to sneak into the park undetected, or was this more recent? Carefully, I pushed through, holding my breath as the whole park came into view.

The Fairgrounds looked as though they had hosted a brutal battle. Clothing littered the open expanse, blowing in the breeze. They were anchored by something. The immediate danger struck me as I heard the sound of wind chimes in the distance. Turning toward the sound, I could see the funhouse directly across from me. I got down on my knees, shielding Leif, but realizing that this vantage point also placed *me* in full view of any hostile forces that could still be lurking here. Leif was getting fidgety and I couldn't afford to let him cry out when the safety of this place was so uncertain. I crept back to the fence line, unwrapped Leif, and put him at my breast. The connection I felt with my son as he fed was indescribable, and it calmed me. Still no sign of life. Perhaps I was alone after all. Perhaps whoever had made this their home had already been killed, and their killers vanished. With that thought, I returned to the opening in the fence that had been my entry point, surveying the grounds for a safe-house among the many buildings. I could creep along the right side of one building and crawl across the grounds. I decided to wait a while longer and attempt the trip under full darkness.

As the darkness engulfed Leif and I, I listened. The wind chimes continued to play as the wind picked up, colder than before. I wrapped my arms around Leif, kissing his head. What happened next made my heart skip a beat.

Chapter Thirty-One

oom! It was the sound of a spotlight turning on, or several. The light fell on the grounds in front of me, highlighting the carnage that had taken place here. Bodies were strewn across the wide expanse of the fairgrounds, frozen in contorted positions between the portable game tents and food stations, all of which were in tatters. I knelt next to the fence and craned my neck around the faux dormer of the haunted house Leif and I were hiding behind. Was this simply a timed event powered by some solar panel, or did it mean something more sinister for us?

Leif was becoming fussy again, upset by the loud noise. I pulled him free of his wrap once more and bounced him on my knee. To my horror he made a face, that face he makes just before he begins to cry. I jabbed my finger in his mouth to silence him, allowing him to suck at it until I managed to pull a breast out of my layered tops, shushing him all the while. He latched to my breast immediately.

"Hungry little monkey, aren't you?" I whispered to him, feeling fortunate that I had this method of calming him if and when the need arose. I often felt pangs of anxiety as I studied his tiny face while he fed. How could I provide for him? Would he survive? The thoughts haunted me mostly at night. Why did I leave the bunker? Destiny, I reminded myself. Leif's destiny is what drove me. I took four deep breaths, exhaling slowly. When Leif was asleep again, I checked his diaper before working him back into his wrap. I had a handful of cloth diapers with me, enough to make it a couple of days before washing became necessary. He was wet, but not wet enough to worry about.

Rolling my neck, I realized just how sore I was all over. As I completed the roll and opened my eyes, what was staring back at me, inches from my face, would have forced a blood curdling scream had I not the presence of mind to stifle it.

A German Shepherd sniffed me up and down, licked its chops and then sat, cocking its head to the side, its expressive eyes on me.

"Hey buddy," I whispered, attempting to smile. I loved dogs and hadn't seen one in a very long time. I was absolutely terrified, but I knew not to show it or the dog might attack. His face was gaunt and his body very skinny. His hair was filthy and knotted. I felt immediately drawn to him. He made a whining sound that broke my heart and pawed at me. I took his paw in my hand and shook it.

"Hi there, puppy." I felt as though I were the one doing the tricks for him. "What's your name?" I whispered, and he again whined.

"You're hungry too, huh?" I reached for my bag and unzipped it. Blindly feeling around I pulled out a package of crackers. "Would you like some of these?" He licked his chops. "Okay," I continued. "Can you lie down?" He did. I gave him four of the saltines. I also pulled a bottle of water and after taking a sip myself poured a portion into a Styrofoam bowl I found on the ground near us. The dog lapped up the water eagerly and I gave him four more crackers.

"You're a good boy, aren't you?" I crooned, patting his head softly. He was in need of companionship as much as food and water, I thought. He licked my hand. I patted him again and rubbed under his chin and neck. He rolled onto his side and then to his back, his paws up in the air.

"Oh, you want a tummy rub too?" I scratched at his belly. He made a squealing sound and leaped up. I pulled away quickly when I realized what I had scratched. It was a gash, an open wound. "Oh no!" I was instantly sad. "Let me see, puppy." I crawled towards him but he backed off licking his nose as he went. "Honey, I want to help, let me see." The dog let out a weak growl, then thought better of it and licked his lips, his head moving from side to side. I didn't want to push my luck, so I backed off. I couldn't be stupid about it: I had Leif on my chest and this was essentially a wild animal now. "If you're sure," I conceded.

He lay down a few feet from me, licked his gruesome wound, and slept. I was concerned that if someone was living in this place they might stumble upon us up here. I ached to get across the grounds to the safety of shelter. But the light: the light left me at an impasse. I curled up on the cold, hard ground with the sack under my head and Leif tight to my body. If it was good enough for our host, the German Shepherd, it would have to be good enough for us.

*****

I awoke with a start. The sun was up. I wasn't surprised that I had let my guard down. Thankfully, I had slept flat on my back, Leif safely strapped to my chest. I sat up and pulled him from the wrap.

"Morning sunshine," I said as he rubbed his eyes and coughed tiny, cute little baby coughs. I muted them against my shirt. "Are you ready to eat something?" I kissed his face about a hundred times and then felt his bum and confirmed a messy morning task ahead.

After changing and feeding Leif, I was ready to assess my situation. The fact that no harm had befallen us all night and the flood lights had extinguished themselves made me confident enough to scout around. Remembering the dog still at my side, I knelt to greet him and patted his head lightly so as not to alarm him. When there was no response I patted a little harder, a sick feeling in my stomach. I put his face in my hands and lifted his snout. I leaned in and put my cheek against his cold, dry nose, trying to detect breath. My bottom lip curled down as a frown formed reflexively on my face. "Oh, no," I squeaked. "Oh, no." My eyes instantly filled with tears. I was surrounded by death. But somehow the loss of an innocent dog, one that had just been alive hours ago, seemed too much.

As I sat next to him, I ran a hand across his bony side, glad that he didn't die alone, starving and thirsty. A tear rolled down my cheek and landed on Leif, who smiled up at me. Why had I brought my helpless son into this heartless world? His smile though, it was irresistible. I was forced to smile back. I would protect him.

*****

Walking along the perimeter of the park, I felt uneasy, like I was being watched. I stopped and slowly sank to the ground, making myself very small. Maybe I should get out of here, continue north. The air was still and no sounds beyond my own breathing were audible. I could say it was *too quiet*, but unless I was walking, Leif was crying, it was raining or the wind was howling, sound was at a minimum these days.

I stood up to better assess the situation. Nothing. Nothing had moved, nothing had disappeared overnight. The fair was as dead as the corpses strewn across its grounds. With a renewed sense of resolve, I made my way carefully across the grounds and into the Fun House, as if something were drawing me there. My heart bursting in anticipation and my head down, I pulled the luggage behind me and passed through the door. Once inside I leaned against a wall and slid slowly down its rough surface.

The walls were all very close, like a labyrinth, and all the mirrors long since smashed or stolen. Just as I was about to move further into the dilapidated building, a crackling sound erupted above me.

"WELCOME, TO CARNIVAL!" A man's voice blared over the loud speaker. I froze.

"WELCOME, TO CARNIVAL!" It repeated. Okay, this could just be a recording, timed to come on just as the lights had.

"YOU SHOULD TRY THE HOTDOGS." Okay, I could breathe again. It *was* a recording. The voice was animated, ridiculous actually. It sounded like a cartoon.

"THEY'RE MADE WITH 100% REAL MEAT. JUST LIKE YOU." *Shit!*

"PLEASE, STEP OUT OF THE FUN HOUSE AND INTRODUCE YOURSELF."

I stood stock still. Panic rose like bile in my throat. There was nowhere to go. I was trapped.

"NO PROBLEM, WE'LL COME TO YOU." *We'll?* There was more than one? Instinct told me to once again make myself very small. I fell to the floor, covering Leif. I realized I was kneeling on something that cut sharply into my knee. My hand instinctively grabbed for it. It was a latch, recessed into the thick plywood. I pulled at it and yanked up hard, pulling a trapdoor loose. I peered blindly into the dark abyss. Seeing a ladder, I climbed down as fast as I could, securing the trapdoor above me.

Trembling, I pulled a flashlight from my pocket and panned it around the tiny space. No more than six feet high and maybe another eight feet long by six feet wide: little more than the dimensions of a grave.

As I was checking the sleeping Leif with my light, I heard the front door snap off its hinges and fall hard many feet from the entrance. I killed the flashlight and buried Leif's head into my neck, covering his ears. I shook uncontrollably as I pressed my back into the dirt corner of the secret room.

"It *was* a girl right?" The man had a heavy voice, thick with thirst. "I would like to see a *girl* again."

"It was a *girl,* Thor," said another, smaller voice. Thor, I thought. Maybe he was the Strong Man in the carnival? I pictured the upturned mustache, the bald head and the heart tattoo on his shoulder.

"Let's split up," suggested the small voice. "We can cover more ground that way."

"Okay." They stomped off in different directions.

Neither of their voices resembled that of the man on the loudspeaker. That meant at least three men lived in the fairgrounds. Neither were immediately above me at this moment but I knew they might only be gone for seconds. If they knew about this room, surely they would have checked here first. Was I safe for the moment?

With that, the footsteps came crashing back and stopped just above me. "We *have* to find her."

Dust poured through the spaces between the plywood slabs as he jostled around. I waved a hand above me to keep the dirt from Leif.

They couldn't capture us, I reasoned desperately. Leif had a great purpose to fulfill and these starving savages could not alter that course.

"I don't see her *anywhere*." The small voice reentered the Fun House as well. Suddenly there was a loud crash above me. One of them had fallen. Had they tripped on the latch?

"What's this?" I heard agitation.

"It's a *bag!*" shouted Thor. I could hear the zipper being ripped open and a great sigh coming from both men. "Holy shit! It's full of food and water."

They laughed together for a time as I silently cried for Leif and I. We would be utterly destitute without it. We couldn't go far without water at the very least. Then I remembered. I wasn't completely helpless - I had a gun hidden in my waistband. It was never far from my body.

"Wait!" ordered the small voice. "Let's eat what we want now and then take the rest back to split with the Master."

"I think we ought to just take it all back. But let's hurry: I'm starving."

"What about the girl?"

"She's gone," thundered the big voice.

"We don't know that. We shouldn't leave here without her."

"We didn't *find* her, so she *must* be gone, must have snuck out."

They seemed to be leaving the Fun House, dragging my sack behind them.

"Listen! We haven't looked *long* enough. If we go back now with just the bag he'll be pissed." The little voice was spiked with fear.

"Fine, but I'm eating something while we wait."

"That's all I'm saying."

I crept silently up the ladder and raised the trapdoor. I could see that my interpretation of what they would look like was not far off the mark. The Strong Man was not so much muscle as just plain huge, but the other man was all of three feet tall. They stood on the veranda. A semi-transparent yellow corrugated plastic roof let the light pour in, while the wooden side walls offered them the privacy they seemed to require. Their *Master* must be watching them from above.

I crawled out of the secret room and got to my feet, setting the door down carefully. I raised the gun, white-knuckled, and pointed it at the Strong Man. I hated the idea of killing anyone like this, in cold blood, but letting our precious bag of food go was not an option.

"What's this?" complained the Strong Man. "Fucking *baby* food?" He held the tin up to the little man. The midget, bearded and dressed in something that resembled a young girl's summer dress with a belt around the middle, looked longingly at the tin.

"A *baby*!" he exclaimed. "Now, that would be a treat!" The tall man grinned evilly, saliva dripping from his toothless mouth, his tongue extending out in a sickening thrashing action.

I shot him first, having decided that he was more of a threat to me than the little man. I hit him in the shoulder and he cried out, dropping the tin. He turned toward me, his eyes squinting against the darkness. What he saw next would be a bright orange flash as I pulled the trigger again and hit him square in the chest. His chest heaved up and down twice as he fell backwards, letting out a final cry as he hit the ground with a thunderous thud, dust rushing out from under him.

My gun was trained on the little man next. His hands were up and eyes wide.

"Listen-" he began. I fired several times, approaching with each squeeze of the trigger. His tiny body convulsed as the bullets pierced his torso. He fell onto his back, arms out, bleeding. The parched wooden porch sponged up the blood thirstily as it exited his lifeless shell.

I had made a lot of noise, so I instantly gathered up Leif and then the bag and ran for it. How many bullets did I have left? How many did a pistol like this hold? I knew it had a magazine, and I knew I had two more just like it full of bullets. But I had no idea how many bullets one held. How many had fired off? Five? Six? Once I had Leif back at my chest I zipped up the bag and peeked beyond the wall.

Chapter Thirty-Two

I had proven that I could kill out of necessity. I looked down at the two Carnies in disgust. The blood bubbled from the Strong Man's chest as air escaped his lungs. I was a much better shot than I had given myself credit for. I had no sympathy for people who saw no other recourse than to eat other people. Sure, the thought had crossed my mind. What if we ran out of food? But the idea for me was unimaginable. I would starve to death first.

I peered again around the corner of the veranda, praying that I wasn't being watched, praying that the *Master* hadn't heard the shots. Not wanting to face him with only one or two bullets left in my gun, I reached into the side pocket of my bag and pulled out a fresh magazine. Releasing the old magazine, I placed it in the luggage pocket and jammed the new one up into the handle of the gun. I pulled back on the barrel until I heard the click. I was ready.

"WELCOME TO CARNIVAL," the loud speaker proclaimed again. I jumped at the voice.

"YOU HAVE BESTED THE *STRONG MAN* AND *SIDEKICK*," he continued. I felt a heat rise across my neck, cheeks and temples.

"ALLOW ME TO INTRODUCE MYSELF. I AM THE RING MASTER. YOU'VE GUESSED BY NOW THAT ALL THE ANIMALS ARE GONE, CONSUMED MANY MONTHS AGO.

THE CLOWNS WERE NEXT, AND THEN THE BUSKERS AND SO ON.”

“IT WAS THE *FREAKS* THAT SURVIVED, UNDER MY GUIDANCE. AND NOW, TO BE BESTED BY A LITTLE GIRL WITH A GUN… *SHAME ON US*.”

This guy was long gone, a long time ago. The patients were running the asylum, so to speak. I pictured him surrounded by human remains somewhere in a little room that overlooked the fairgrounds.

I set down my bag and was deliberating on what to do next when the speakers crackled on again.

“I WOULD VERY MUCH LIKE TO MEET YOU.”

It was an invitation to dinner, no doubt. Where Leif and I would be the main course.

“I WILL BE DOWN MOMENTARILY.” Then the speakers went dead. Again, silence. I had to act, or take cover. I panicked a moment, unsure of how to face this enemy. He was clearly nuts. He had probably been so since the moment he swallowed human flesh for the first time. I wondered which direction he might be coming from. It was impossible to tell. The speakers carried throughout the park. I looked toward the front gates. No one. Then I looked toward the back of the park, where an amphitheatre, five stories tall, acted as the focal point. Rows of seating overlooked a central dirt pad where, I guessed, the Ring Master ran his Circus.

Suddenly, a violent breeze had picked up the dirt, swirling it in the air. The roar of an engine echoed off the seating, the amphitheatre magnifying the sound. It was deafening.

If his intention was to scare the living shit out of me, mission accomplished. It sounded like he was riding some hellish creation with seven mufflers, eight wheels and an open engine. I was stuck in place, my nails digging into the wooden wall. I couldn’t take my eyes off the spectacle. He tore down the grounds toward me, running over the corpses, crashing through the dilapidated food stations and games tents.

I pulled myself away from the vision, backing off into the Fun House. I thought about hiding underground once more, but the idea of being trapped there with no escape plan save shooting my way out frightened me just as much as facing him head on.

The vehicle rushed past me, spewing dust onto the veranda. It was obnoxiously loud. He began circling the Fun House entrance in quick successive right turns. On closer inspection of the vehicle, I could see it was some kind of motorcycle with two massive wheels in the back and one in the front, connected to the bike by a long chrome leg. The man's appearance was blurred by the amount of dust and dirt he was kicking up. Likely a tactic he was using to flush me out. Instead, I decided to take aim.

Leif was crying at my chest, still attached via the sling I'd made over two months before. I curled both hands around my pistol and fired recklessly into the circle of flying debris. I counted my shots until the barrel stopped firing. The motorcycle continued to circle outside the front entrance.

I pulled out another clip, palmed it up inside the handle and took aim, but the cycle's circling ceased, the engine whirring at a lower decibel. I stepped cautiously onto the veranda, the smoke and dirt clearing. I squinted my eyes. Was anyone left on the bike? Had I managed to shoot him off? As surreal as the circumstances had become, I flashed back to a childhood memory of the carnival. I'd spent my allowance for that week firing a water rifle at moving targets for most of the afternoon, desperate to win the pink, stuffed pony. Had I won the proverbial pony here?

The smoke had cleared and the bike continued to hum without its rider. Side-stepping to check the far side of the bike for a body, I carefully rounded the back, gun still drawn. *Jesus, Sara! Don't go any further.* The voice in my head was right: why didn't I stop? I had a screaming baby strapped to my chest. But the curiosity and adrenaline had gotten the better of me, and I couldn't seem to stop myself. Leif was wailing – the deafening gunshots had probably hurt his ears, hopefully not irrevocably, but I dared not set him down. I ignored his pleas to be coddled. I needed to end this twisted chapter in my trip.

"I will blow your head off!" I blindly threatened the Ring Master over Leif's frightened cries.

As the far side of the bike came into view I saw the man, curled over on his side, arms crossed over his stomach, rocking back and forth. He wore leather chaps over faded jeans and cowboy boots whose soles had long since fallen off. His torso was bare save a cape he had tied around his neck. It was his face though which captured my interest. Nothing should have surprised me anymore. But this did.

He wore a red rubber clown's nose torn down the center. His eyebrows were gone. Deep scars split his cheeks, travelling from the corner of each eye down to his jaw. His head was covered in a ridiculous orange fuzzy wig. He looked up at me, and as he did blood rushed out of his mouth, mixing with the dusty earth. He tried to say something through a painted smile.

I shot him in the chest without hesitation. Blood splattered across the ground as his heart exploded from the impact. His head fell hard and fast, his eyes staring into the abyss. Whatever he had to say to me I didn't want to hear. I lowered my arm and spun around, careful not to leave myself vulnerable to another attack.

Then the immensity of what had happened hit me like a ton of bricks. My face hurt as it contorted and I screamed out, stomping my feet. Leif was stunned momentarily into silence, and then cried harder than before. I knew I had to get away. I couldn't be in this place any longer. The motor bike was still running and I thought it looked simpler than a regular motorcycle to operate. I looked the machine up and down. I had ridden dirt bikes before, and this couldn't be much different. I grabbed my bag, tied it down to the wide back rack and climbed on. Leif continued to protest, but getting us free of the carnival was my priority.

I pushed down on the clutch, revved the handle and toed at the gears. I popped the clutch when I had decided I was in first and jerked forward. I was moving! I pushed the clutch again and toed at the gears to second and rallied through the grounds on approach to the front gates. Slamming through the maintenance gate, I made a hard right following my original path, heading north. Whatever lay to the north, it couldn't be worse than this.

Chapter Thirty-Three

I drove the entire day, stopping in spurts to feed Leif and myself. The freedom I experienced riding in the open air was exhilarating. The wind in my face and hair, billowing against my jacket and long pants offered a welcome reprieve from the world at large. I was able to reconnect briefly with a younger me, who used to ride my father's dirt bike in the field adjacent to our house. Leif was lulled to sleep by the motion each time we got back on the road. I kept my speed to a minimum in order to conserve gas, never actually turning it off as we stopped, for fear of it never starting again. I worried about the level of noise the bike created but convinced myself that it would accelerate our path to Leif's destiny. Who knew how long I had until I got to where I was going.

That's the thing about destiny. It seems to know where you're headed, even if you don't. So I assumed we were heading to something, somewhere, north. The devastated landscape was little more than an endless graveyard of rotting forests, still ponds and fields of radioactive dirt. As I moved past them, the forward motion in my peripheral blurred the scenery into torn grey curtains. If others had headed north on this highway, they had done so long ago. There was no sign of life on the road.

*****

After roughly eight hours on the deserted highway I hit a wall. I was exhausted, my eyes burned, and my arms ached from navigating the bike around countless obstacles. Even my back throbbed from the angle I was forced to sit at. I followed the first off-ramp I came to, located a rest stop, and pulled in. Hesitantly I pushed the red stop button on the bike's dash. If it started again, great, but if it didn't I guessed I could chalk that up to destiny. All I knew was that I couldn't ride it anymore. As I stepped off the bike all the blood seemed to rush back into my thighs, igniting a pain so severe it felt as though I had run the whole way. I rubbed my legs and arched my torso, palms pushing against my lower back. Leif remained comfortably in his wrap strapped to my chest, sleeping.

It wasn't a truck stop or anything elaborate, but it met our needs and I was thankful for it. A rest stop this far north normally had a well that could be manually pumped for clean water. This stop was also small enough to be overlooked by most. Though it may offer water, it would offer little else, I noted. Even the information building had been vandalized beyond recognition for the contents of its vending machines.

All I needed was water, and some semblance of shelter.

As I inspected my new surroundings I slipped the pistol out of my waistband. Though the odds seemed remote that I should run into another hostile survivor in this isolated place, the idea of it still spooked me. What looked like birch trees stood along the perimeter of the rest stop, their tops missing. Nothing green remained. A wind had picked up from the south and I flinched as it rattled the dead branches and carried debris down the highway. I cursed its timing.

I crept up to a sign at the end of the parking lot that read *Historic Site, 1814. Site of the James Spring Reservoir, established to aid troops in the war of blah blah blah*… I wondered if future generations would plant signs like these in the hot spots of the world created by the Reaper's evil deed. What I was hoping for with the sign was some indication that a well was near. I spun around and sighed. I had already drained a half dozen bottles of water and needed to replenish them. I had to keep my fluids up. Leif's dependency on my breast milk made this a tantamount necessity.

Suddenly, a new sound, and I froze. Branches again, snapping, but not in the way the wind would push the tree tops and snap them. This snapping was consistent and *deliberate*. The forest was alive with the sound. Someone or something was walking through the woods. I strained my eyes against the encroaching twilight but saw nothing. Then a loud crunch came from behind the ravaged information building.

Whatever it was must not have seen us yet. It definitely came from behind the building. I ran back to my bike on the balls of my feet and mounted it once more. I made myself small, leaning over the gas tank, kneeling on the seat, my gun trained on the far side of the building. Amazingly, Leif was still sleeping. I waited for the sound's creator to emerge.

After several tense seconds, the head of a deer poked around the corner of the ruined building. I was struck by its huge, sad eyes. Its tongue licked at its nose as it stepped out into the parking lot. I remained still, not wanting to scare her. My gun followed her as she moved across the lot and left. The poor thing was emaciated and moved painfully slowly. What had she been living on all this time? Bark? As much as I loved animals, I was no vegetarian and a slab of venison cooking over an open fire flashed in my mind. My mouth automatically watered. I could kill this deer if it was truly life or death. But I had food, I didn't need to kill for anything yet. The bigger question would be how would I skin it and cut it up? Then a vision of Earl *skinning* Gareth forced the thought from my mind. I continued to follow the doe with my eyes as it moved into the woods. I watched as she nosed at a short stump. As she did, the right side of the narrow stump gave way and lifted. She did this several times before I realized what was happening. It was no stump- it was a water pump!

I dismounted the bike once more and slowly approached the doe. The sound of liquid hitting the ground was music to my ears. The pump was producing water! I let the deer drink what water had collected in the cement basin and watched it go. Then I ran to the pump, lifted the arm and pushed down. I did this until the water gushed out of the spout. I leaned down, cupped my hands together until they were full of water. Then I drank deeply. It was good. I ran back to the bike, collected my bottles from the bag, and refilled them.

*****

That night Leif and I settled into the information building. I ate a meal of crackers, canned carrots and canned pineapple, drinking all the water I could stomach. I was so happy to have found a water source, I decided to stay near it as long as no one discovered us.

For about three days after arriving at the rest stop I awoke to the deer at the pump, its squeaking handle bringing me out of a restless sleep. I would trudge to the well, Leif in tow, and fill my bottles to capacity. Our days were spent sleeping, eating, and occasionally playing. Leif was able to respond to my smiles now. His toothless grin could entertain me for hours on end. I would sing to him and tell him I loved him. Thank God this little person had come into my life.

On the fourth day, I started to realize what I was doing. Was it unhealthy to be so attached to the pump, to the water? Was it counter-productive? Who knew if I'd ever find a water source like that again? Afraid to relinquish this link to life, I chewed at my fingernails absent-mindedly, spitting the gnarled nails out and examining the finger tips. Was this a problem? Could I make myself leave? My other hand worked a length of my dark, greasy hair around my index finger as I pondered my dilemma.

This couldn't be Leif's destiny, to grow up here. What sort of destiny would that be? Yet I was so reluctant to get back on the motorcycle and leave the pump that it made me shake to think about it. If I left I was leaving for good. If I left and we never found water again then what? If I stayed and ran out of food the water would only keep us alive for a few days more. So, what would be my catalyst? What would make me leave?

I felt a deep connection with Joel in that moment, understanding what he must have struggled with during those last few weeks. Making life or death decisions on behalf of others was excruciating.

"A little help," I pleaded aloud in a whisper, looking up at the grey sky above. The low-lying clouds moved quickly overhead. "Storm," I said. September storms, they were a force. Joel had loved a storm in *life*. I had learned to love them too. But alone, vulnerable and with a newborn, a storm meant hardships never before imagined. A rain drop hit my nose and I ran inside, Leif in my arms. There were no doors left on the building to close behind me, and if the rain fell in any direction other than straight down we would be soaked in seconds. The structure was little more than a booth and had lost all of its windows to looters a long time ago. The rain began, falling hard on the metal roof. It fell in sheets within a minute. A wind blew into the building, spraying the rain all over me. I sucked in a breath unconsciously and turned my back on it, trying to keep Leif dry.

"Shit," I whispered as a chill ran through me. As warm as the morning was, the rain felt wintery cool against my face and hands. Leif began to cry, the shock of the icy rain on his skin a rude awakening.

The wind picked up in intensity, blowing more of the rain into the building. I might as well have been standing in the middle of the parking lot for all the shelter I was getting. I shifted, moving back and forth in the tiny building, hoping for more shelter, but none was to be found. I was dripping wet in minutes. The roar of the rain pounding on the roof was deafening, and a crash of thunder exploded overhead, Leif screamed into my ear. I was freezing, shaking uncontrollably, praying for the storm to pass.

All at once, as quickly as it had taken me from bone dry to soaking wet, the rain stopped and a glimmer of sun pierced the cloud. Now, I knew something about northern storms in September and I knew that this was merely a taste of what was to come. I knew of no other possible shelter in the area. This building was it. Even the tiny washroom which I'd huddled into had no door left to shut. My blankets were soaked. If this kept up all day I'd have a very uncomfortable night. Perhaps this ought to have been my catalyst. Maybe I could outrun the storm on the bike?

Leif had been crying since the initial spray of windswept rain had woken him. I think I was crying too. I bounced him while I paced back and forth, considering my options. Was leaving too rash a decision?

"Fine." I stopped myself and held Leif under his arms, lifting him to my face. He stared at me with sad eyes. "I'm going to ask you a question, and then give you two possible answers. If you make a noise after I offer the answer then we will follow that path. Understand?"

"Leif," I said in a low tone. "What do you think we should do? Stay?" I waited for the crying to begin, but he remained silent.

"Go?"

He whimpered immediately.

I wasn't going to question Leif's destiny; if he was meant to stay that was not the answer I got. I picked up my wrap and fitted him inside, slung it over my shoulder, grabbed my bag, and secured it to the bike.

My water supply was full save a couple of bottles, but if I was going to beat the storm north I had to move. Looking to the pump, I smiled, blew it a kiss and pushed the ignition button on the bike. It rumbled to life. My heart soared and we navigated back onto the highway, continuing north.

Chapter Thirty-Four

I had managed to keep far enough ahead of the growing storm clouds to pull over and change out of my wet clothes. The artificial wind in my face caused my teeth to chatter and my skin to tighten. It was a chilling experience, like being tossed into a lake in early spring. I noticed Leif could use a change as well and pulled over. I dug through the contents of the giant bag secured to the bike's back rack, pulling out a new onesie and a full set of pajamas. I had become masterfully quick at the process of changing the baby. He was usually happy to accommodate me too. He appreciated the luxury of a clean diaper and fresh clothes.

Once we were both dry and dressed, I climbed back onto the three-wheeler and pushed on, looking over my shoulder constantly. My anxiety increased as the clouds advanced behind us.

I squinted against the speed-induced wind as an alarming thought struck. What if I were to come across the mass grave Earl, Sonny and Freddy claimed to have stumbled upon months before? I would see it long before I came to it. The roads now were straight and flat, the hills on the horizon always a distant marker. I couldn't even be sure whether I was on the same highway. All I knew for sure was my direction: north. The compass on the bike offered that small reassurance.

*****

Three hours into my journey, the storm clouds a distant memory and the sky above me only blue, the bike's fuel light began to blink wildly. Ten minutes later I was pushing the bike into a ditch.

My bag resting on its wheels, the handle extended and my baby strapped to my torso, I once again felt terribly vulnerable as I grasped the bag and moved forward on unsteady legs. I walked roughly three more hours before coming to a deep valley. The angle of decline was extreme but I continued onward, digging my heels into the asphalt. My bag kept clipping at my ankles so I pulled it out in front of me, its weight pulling me off center. 'Don't fall, don't fall, don't fall...' I repeated aloud. It took an enormous amount of concentration to finally arrive safely at the bottom of the valley. But it was at the base that I felt the most insecure. Looking down at my feet, I saw that I was standing in a small stream. The water was still, the banks had flooded from what must have been a torrential downpour similar to that which chased me from my well. A ripple hit my ankle, approaching from my right. Then a second later, another. My heart lodged in my throat. There was absolutely no wind in the valley. It could be another animal, I surmised, perhaps a frog, or small fish that had survived in this muck? But my gut told me it was something else, *someone* else.

Not wanting to look up and confirm my fear, I kept my eyes on the water. The ripples became more frequent, followed by the sound of legs dragging in knee-high water. I reached into my waistband slowly, fingers wrapping around the handle of the pistol and gingerly pulling it free. I looked to my right, straining to see what the fates had thrown at me this time. The sound suddenly increased in volume and speed. I turned to face the noise with my pistol raised and ready.

Two men mere moments from tackling me stopped dead in their tracks, their arms raised over their heads automatically. One was much older than the other. He looked eighty-five but probably was no more than sixty. The other man, who appeared to be in his early twenties gestured wildly in surrender, backing away. The old man produced a long knife from his sleeve and turned it in his fingers.

"Now, now, pretty lady. All we want is what you have." He inched closer. The young man eyed him.

"What I have is my own," I retorted. "You come any closer and I'll shoot you!"

"Now, now," he continued as he slowly stepped up onto the road. "You don't want to shoot me. You're a nice little girl." At that I cocked the hammer and again he froze in place.

"I've killed men before." I cleared my throat so as not to seem so terrified. "I've killed before and I will kill you where you stand." Trying not to let my hands shake, I thrust the gun further in front of me.

His head cocked and his brows rose. "Oh, I don't believe that." His mouth widened to a smile under his unkempt beard. "I doubt there are even any bullets in your gun. Mine hasn't seen a bullet in over a year."

"I'm not kidding. I *will* shoot you!" I shouted. My voice was shaky. Had I changed the magazine after I took down the clown? All this time I'd just assumed the gun had been loaded. My heart pounded angrily in my chest, my face flushed, my eyes narrowed to slivers.

"I think you're mistaken," he said, resuming his approach.

"Only one way to find out," I said with what confidence I could muster. The man's eyes widened and he lunged towards me, arm shooting up to bring the knife down. I fired twice. To my attacker's amazement, he fell backwards as each bullet caught him in his midsection. He landed with a splash in the knee-high water beside the road and sank to its filthy bottom. I trained the gun on his young friend next.

"Dad!" He yelped before running to pull him out of his watery grave. He looked wildly up at me. "You killed him!"

"What did you think I would do?" I shouted back, shaking. "I have a *baby*!" It was a horrible thing - a son watching his father die - but I was someone's mother now. *Leif's* mother. And I would not let anyone harm him.

"You bitch!" His voice gave out and he sank to his knees beside his father's shallow grave. It had occurred to me that I ought to shoot him too, so he would not follow me and attack us in the night.

"You stay," I told him as I grabbed the handle of my bag and moved backwards. "You just stay where you are and you'll be fine." He didn't respond for a time. I was half way up the other side of the valley highway before he realized I'd gone.

"You!" he screamed as he spotted me. My gun, returned to my waistband for the trip up, slipped through my loose pants and tumbled down the hill as I struggled to retrieve it. Knowing that my only chance was to outrun him, I dropped my bag and raced the rest of the way up the steep hill, Leif crying at my chest. Looking back, I saw to my horror that he was tearing up the hill after me, with *my* gun in hand. Reaching the top of the valley, I ran headfirst into the waiting arms of a stranger.

Chapter Thirty-Five

I heard my gun go off before I was immediately hustled into the back of a parked truck. I remember telling the men that I had a baby, and needed help. They understood that all too well, shooting down my assailant as he appeared at the crest of the hill. He was cut down by the gun mounted to the roof of a jeep. The man whose body I had plowed into jumped into the back of the truck with me. He, like his companions, wore a face mask and combat fatigues. I guessed that this was the military. This was the rescue we'd all hoped for in the beginning. I felt I'd come full circle. There were six of them in total.

"Let me see your neck and your torso," ordered the hollow voice behind the mask.

"My torso?" I wondered whether I was really safe after all.

"We need to inspect you. Are you feverish? How's your eyesight?"

"I-I'm fine," I stammered. "My eyesight is fine. What do you need to see on my torso?" It was difficult shouting back and forth with the baby crying.

"Precautions. We check all unknowns for the plague before they are admitted."

"Admitted to what?"

"The base. Now remove your shirt."

"I have a baby strapped to my chest. Could you please relax?" I slowly pulled Leif out of his worn sling and placed him lovingly down on the metallic truck bed. I then pulled off my top layers, my bra catching on the last of them and a sliver of my white breast popping out. My elbow instinctively snapped into a defensive position, covering the nipple.

"You look fine," he concluded, sensing my embarrassment. "I mean, free of spots. The plague." He struggled with his words.

My brows raised. *Never seen a nipple before?* "Okay, now what?"

"Let me see your baby." He reached out. I picked Leif up and reluctantly handed him over to the soldier. An intense anxiety overcame me. I gathered up my tops and held them in a bunch in front of me.

After undressing him, he gave Leif a thorough visual inspection. "How old?"

"About two months." I answered.

"Little small for two months, isn't he?"

"He was a month or two premature."

He handed Leif back to me and I dressed him quickly.

"What now?" I asked again.

He lowered his mask. "Now we can take you to the base." He gave us a broad and reassuring smile. I couldn't help noticing that he was incredibly handsome. "I'm Sergeant Jones, by the way."

"I'm Sara, and this is Leif." I felt suddenly hot and ran my hands over my rib cage feeling uncomfortably aware of my state of undress.

"Good to meet you both," he grinned, his eyes wandering a moment to my chest, and then to the baby. "I'll see to it you are well cared for upon our return." He stepped down from the truck bed.

"I guess I should thank you for saving my life," I smiled back. He turned and nodded, then tapped the side of the truck and it roared to life.

"I'll follow you back."

Part Two
Chapter Thirty-Six

The base was a modern marvel. It used wind and solar power for virtually all of its energy needs. There were fifteen windmills jutting up into the sky some sixty feet from a central point along with hundreds of solar panels attached to the roofs of the common buildings.

In a way, the base was an upgrade to what we had had at Joel's house. There, we had run power off the generator that ran on fuel and had our own well, but that was it. Joel's cold storage, though essential to our survival, was a miniature version of what the base had hidden beneath the floors of the kitchen: massive freezers and clean rooms that were stocked with dried meat, fruit, vegetables, canned and boxed goods. Enough to last two hundred people for fifty years, they told me. When I arrived at the base, there were only eighty-six people.

One of my favorite things about the base was the animals. I had missed animals, hugging them, playing with them. The base had a large metal barn that housed some twenty cattle, fourteen goats, probably fifty chickens and a couple of pigs. But when the pigs refused to mate, they instead became pets. *One day we'll just eat them,* the Sergeant said once, but his children loved the pigs and he could never put them on a plate in front of them.

The base also drew its water from underground wells. The water was then treated with ultraviolet light, charcoal filters and a variety of other filters before it ever made it to our mouths. They had a brilliant grey water recycling system as well. Rain water was collected and used for the toilets and for washing. It was literally a Shangri-la in the midst of a terrible desert.

The walls, which reached a height of twenty feet in places, were outfitted with watch towers. There was also a stockade, family housing, a mess hall, hospital and the central training and parade grounds. This base even included a greenhouse.

Our daily lives consisted of keeping the base running smoothly. Everyone's unique skills were put to good use, and I had been employed in many capacities, the last three years dedicating all of my time to the hospital.

Eight years had passed since I first drove through the gates in the back of that truck, my heart in my throat. This was where my son grew up. It was more a home to me than anything I'd known since the Reaper struck and the *only* home Leif had ever known. Though the grey on grey treatment to the buildings interiors was bleak, and the military precision as to how things were run felt a little claustrophobic at times, the alternative to living here was not an alternative at all.

We had been given a shower, disinfected, administered shot after shot and issued five sets of clothes each, all within our first hour inside the base. Leif had been doted over by the women here, many of the nurses becoming my close friends within the first month, the doctor a source of great comfort.

I counted my blessings and lived each day grateful for the abundance of food, water, and people. I hadn't realized just how much I missed meeting new people.

Leif attended a school daily and grew up happy, oblivious to the world I had grown up in. It was just as well, as this world was still a mess. There were still no leaves on the trees, no grass in the fields. No nothing. My hope for a future was waning for Leif, but I remained outwardly positive.

I watched him run into our bunkroom and jump up onto his bed. He reminded me so much of his father. The way he smiled at me. His eyes were the same, and I imagined that when he got older, he would have Joel's lean muscular physique. But there was something about my son that went beyond physical features in their similarities. An eerie recognition. Often a cloud of anxiety overtook me when he stared at me. He'd lie on his bed and stare across the room at me while I read.

"What is it, baby?" I would ask, looking up from my book.

"Nothing, Mom," was his reply. It was as though he was trying to work out some great mystery in his head. He looked so thoughtful. Sometimes he didn't even realize I was staring back.

"Mom," he asked once, "was I born here?"

"Nope, not here."

"Then where, then?"

"Why do you want to know, sweetheart?"

"Some of the other kids were telling each other where they were born and I said I was born here because that's where they were saying they were born."

I sat up and spun around to face him. Our cots were just three feet apart and separated by a night table. The lights in the building flickered. "You were born just a couple of days drive south of here."

"Can we go see?"

"Not without an escort."

"Oh, so it's dangerous?"

"Probably."

"Will I ever be allowed to go there?"

"Why do you need to?"

"I was talking to Blank Man. He said I would go there one day. I just wondered if we could go tomorrow."

My heart always sank at the name, *Blank Man*. Leif claimed he was a figure that would visit him, a man who occasionally gave him advice and helped him with his school work.

"*Blank Man* huh?" It had been eight years since my witches had identified his presence, saying he was attached to my son.

"I know you don't like him, Mom. He told me that too."

"He doesn't think I like him? Why is that?"

"Because you don't," he said matter-of-factly and tucked himself under the covers.

"I never *said* that."

"You never had to." He rolled over and coughed. "Goodnight, Mom."

"Goodnight, Leif." He was so intuitive. Or was that *Blank Man* whispering into his ear? I took a deep breath and closed my textbook, its cover filled with illustrations of combat injuries.

The idea that Joel's angel, *our* angel, was one and the same as this *Blank Man* my son spoke of still sent a shiver through me. It's visits were becoming more and more frequent, and all I could do was hope that something positive developed.

Chapter Thirty-Seven

I walked to the mess hall at 7:00 am to pick up my food and water ration, my mind running through the conversation I'd had with my son the night before. From the mess hall I went to the post-op where three men were recovering from wounds acquired during a raid that left some of the base's solar panels damaged.

"Hi Sarge," I greeted Sergeant Jeffery Jones, who was recovering from shrapnel wounds. The same man who had saved our lives eight years ago. "How's that knock you took on the head feel today?"

"I'm fine, Sara." He was a tough one. All the men and women here were the toughest people I'd ever met. Tough, but also smart.

"Glad to hear it. But don't try sneaking out of here just yet. The doctor wants to check that gash this morning."

"Yes, sir!" he replied with a wink and a smile. I liked him. If he weren't married, I would have scooped him up years ago. He'd be forty-four the following month but didn't look a day over thirty. He and I had our routine: flirt, flirt back. My face flushed a little every time, and I knew he liked that. He was exceptionally handsome, and just my type. The more I got to know him, the more I liked him. I feared I was beginning to lose the ability to just flirt.

"Thirty-five stitches and no local." I read his update. "Who are you trying to impress!" I smiled as I replaced his chart and moved to the next bed where a drifter, picked up west of here a month ago, laid on his side, his left leg badly mangled. "And how are you faring, Brad?"

"Been better." His smile was pained. "Maybe I should have let them leave me to my own devices." The army sent patrols out in search of drifters within a ten mile radius every week while hunting local terrorists. Of course Brad chose to join our group: left to your own devices meant left to die, eventually.

"Stay off that leg," I smiled. The patients seemed to take to my bedside manner. Perhaps in *life* I would have made a good doctor. Having studied with the local hospital in my last year of high school, I was grateful for what real life experience I'd gained.

That seemed like a lifetime ago.

"Sara," whispered Jeffrey from his cot. "How's Don doing?"

Don was the third patient in the far bunk. He'd been shot in the chest and lost a lot of blood. We pulled plasma from every available resident as often as we could, but lately we'd been going through it fast.

"He's still in a coma. Dr. Bren doesn't think he'll snap out of it any time soon either." I looked at Don, and bit at my lower lip. "He won't keep him on support much longer."

"Understood." Don and Jeffrey were good friends. Don had been shot over a week earlier on a patrol. It had been a mad frenzy when they brought him in. I hated to see the Sergeant so crestfallen. But understanding our limited resources was something we all had to come to terms with, in every aspect of our lives.

"He may yet pull through." Why did I say that? It was in my nature to comfort others. I knew Don had no chance.

"Thanks for saying that, Sara. You know, guys like Don are important now, more than ever," he began. "If good people don't survive, then our very humanity dies."

That was profound. I repeated those words in my head.

"Sorry, I shouldn't have said that."

"No, that was a beautiful statement."

"Still, I …" His head pushed back into his pillow and he closed his eyes.

"You never know, Jeff." I placed a hand on his forearm and squeezed. He smiled up at me, eyes still shut.

I left the recovery room and headed for the operating room, where I would sterilize the tools and wash down the floors. En route I slowed and stopped in the hall. I felt weak, my eyelids fluttering frantically. Then I was suddenly overcome by emotion, tears streaming down my cheeks. Upon wiping them from my face, the tears flowed freely, as though I'd just poked a hole in my own defenses. I cried silently to myself in the empty hall for a few moments before regaining my composure and carrying on. It was what I had learned to do. Just carry on.

Chapter Thirty-Eight

A fter a modest dinner with my son in the mess hall, we watched a movie in the nursery with the other moms and their children. The kids sat up front while the women talked in low whispers behind them. I almost always sat with Adrienne, Sergeant Jones' wife. She had managed to create a school, and teach all grades single-handedly, while overseeing the nursery, and helping the one chef train an army of cooks. She was a woman of boundless energy, and I respected her immensely. But on top of that, she had won the Sergeant's love and affection, and I think that meant more to me than all of her successes. She was a smart and modest woman. She wondered how, after hearing my story, I could hold anyone's achievements above my own. She made me feel accomplished, as did her husband. Though she held no rank, and Jeffrey was only a Sergeant, they were the power couple on the base. That was unquestioned.

After the movie, we all returned to our bunks. Lights out was 10 pm to allow the batteries to charge over night. Once there I felt a gnawing urge to question Leif on his apparitions. So while I got him ready for bed, I did.

"What does the *Blank Man* look like, Leif?"

"He's tall and shiny around the edges."

"What about his face, honey?" I pressed.

"I don't know." He fidgeted with his shoes.

"Well, does he look like anyone we know? Does he look like Sergeant Jones? Or maybe he looks a little like the Chaplain?"

"Is his hair dark, light, does he have hair? Is his nose long or short? Is he..."

"He said he'd have a face when I gave him one," he interrupted, looking up at me. "That's why I call him Blank Man." Leif returned his attention to his shoes.

That description rattled me. I unfolded his pajama top and pulled it over his head. *"He's dark,"* is how Carol had described him.

"Why is he here, Leif? Does he want something from you?" It seemed as good a time as any to get into it. I knew he was watching us, but as yet, no reason had presented itself as to why beyond the shroud of destiny.

"I don't know, Mom. It's just Blank Man."

"He hasn't given you any reason why he's here?"

"No."

"Leif." I adopted a more authoritative tone. "I'm asking these questions because I love you. Can you *really* not tell me why the *Blank Man* is here?"

"No. It's a secret, Mom, and I don't want to break a promise."

"A secret," I repeated. That made the hairs on the back of my neck stand on end. A sudden urge to protect him overwhelmed me.

"Leif, do you *love* me?"

"Yes."

"Then you shouldn't keep secrets from me should you?"

"But Blank Man said…"

"Forget what *Blank Man* said. If you love me you won't keep secrets from me."

"Okay." He shot a look behind me and to my left. I quickly turned. Our door was shut, the corner was dark. Turning back to Leif, I asked, "Is he here now? *Blank Man?*"

"Yes."

"Is he speaking to you?"

"Yes."

Jesus. My skin crawled.

"Listen to me, Leif. I'm your mother. No one can tell you what to do but me. You trust me right?"

"Yes, Mom." His eyes were still trained on the corner of the room behind me.

"Then tell *Blank Man* he should go, and leave us alone." I was testing the spirit's resolve. Pushing him to explain his intentions.

"I can't, Mom."

"Why, Leif?"

"Because, Mom." He looked in my eyes. My forehead creased, my eyebrows raised in expectation.

"Just *because?*"

"He says he wants to tell you himself."

"Ask him honey. Ask him to tell me then."

Leif's eyes shot back to the corner by the door.

"He's gone."

"Shit!"

"Mom!"

"Sorry, come here." Leif stood and walked towards me. I motioned for a hug and didn't let go for a very long time.

Chapter Thirty-Nine

D ays later the base was under siege again.

"What's happened?" I asked as I approached the heavy chain link gate that separated us from the outside world. The siren wailed throughout the parade grounds, signaling to the hospital staff that casualties were on their way.

"Looks like they finally did what needed doing," Doctor Bren, jogging beside me, shouted victoriously.

"What was that?" I shouted back, slowing as we made the gate.

"A run-in with those terrorists. They're on their way back with a couple of car loads." Terrorists, that's what they called the marauding bands of misfits that continuously tested our defenses.

"We have casualties?" The question seemed redundant. The fact that we were called to the gate meant someone was hurt.

"Not ours, I hear." Just then the covered truck transporting the prisoners could be seen approaching. But they weren't slowing to allow the gate keeper a chance to properly unchain and open the gates. They were *accelerating*!

"Fall back!" someone called from the tower, and the hospital staff scattered. I landed to the right of the gates and climbed part way up the metal ladder on approach to the tower. As I climbed I watched in horror as the truck slammed through the gates, running down three of our medical staff in cold blood. It came to a sudden halt in the middle of our compound.

Doctor Bren was at the foot of the ladder. He drew his weapon and shot three times into the cab of the truck, sending each shot expertly into the body and head of the driver. I watched as the man slumped over the wheel. A moment of deathly silence followed. The doctor stood with his firearm raised, feet parted while his free arm held the rail of the ladder I was hugging.

Suddenly, men in tattered clothing leaped out of the back of the truck and raced for cover. The doctor ran for cover himself, firing at the men as he waved his medical staff to safety. At this point the tower guards fired down on the intruders. Men exploded on the ground as the rounds connected. Snapping out of my horror-induced daze and realizing just how vulnerable I was, I began climbing the ladder again, shouting over the hum of the machine guns to the tower guard.

Moments later, I saw two more trucks on the horizon moving toward us in a blaze of dust. Was this more of the same? Then I heard the radio crack on in the tower. "Have they made contact with the base yet?" It was Sergeant Jones' voice.

"They have. What the fuck happened out there, Sergeant?!" That was the Captain's voice now.

"They managed to hijack one of our trucks, but we've got their leader with us now and are in hot pursuit." Jeff's voice sounded confident through the static.

"Not hot enough, Sergeant! They've already managed to breach our gate and raise hell. I need your team back here now!"

Within moments Jeffrey's hummer burst into the compound, slamming into the west wall and crushing one of the terrorists into oblivion. I watched as the Sergeant opened his door and jumped out of the vehicle. I prayed he would be okay. Then I stared at the rear window of the hummer. There sat the leader of the terrorist cell. Impossibly, he seemed strangely familiar.

The melee was in full swing when the second hummer cruised into the base to aid in its defense. Four men jumped out of the vehicle and split up in pairs, keeping low to the ground. I couldn't say exactly how many terrorists there were to begin with, but I knew for certain that four of them were very, very dead.

In a flash of terror I saw a man approaching Jeffrey from behind and to the right, narrowly hidden by his parked Hummer. I anxiously tapped out instructions to the gunner in the tower with me, pointing to the target. The gunner nodded, aimed, and fired. The would-be attacker was thrown up against the wall, his left arm torn from his body. Jeffery, oblivious to the near-disaster, shot controlled rounds into another of the invaders making his way into one of the out-buildings. The man slumped quietly to the ground, hand still tightly clenching a door handle.

"Perimeter check!" shouted Jeffrey when all went quiet. The five soldiers stood slowly and crept around the compound for several minutes. Jeffery ordered one of them to secure the covered truck and the rest to drag the dead to a central point on the parade grounds. Our dead were tenderly lifted onto stretchers and raced inside. When we got the "all clear" I descended the ladder on shaky legs. Crossing the compound to enter the hospital, I noticed Jeffrey moving the prisoner out of the Hummer. *"Oh my God…"* I whispered to myself. I *did* recognize him. A quarter of his face burned away, years since I'd laid eyes on him, I could hear his voice in my ear. *Earl.*

Chapter Forty

The military trial was set for Friday. We buried our dead and burned the invaders' bodies, salvaging what could be useful to the base.

I still reeled from the idea that Earl was in such close proximity. Four days after the attack, I wondered whether I ought to visit him, if for no other reason than to gloat. I imagined what I would say to him, the things I would accuse him of at his trial. He hadn't seen me, of that I was sure, or he would have asked for me by now. I had so many questions for him. How did he escape the fire? Was he responsible for Sidney and Caroline's deaths? Did he get that nasty burn because of me? I hoped so.

Sitting in the daycare with Leif and five other children, my mind wandered. I went back to the day we lit the house on fire. Sidney and Caroline were at my side, Leif was just a brand new baby swaddled and hugging my stomach. I could smell the fuel and feel the cold metal cans in my hand as I poured the flammable liquid along the perimeter of the house.

"Mom." Leif was calling me.

"Yes, honey?"

"What's wrong with Sherri?" Sherri was a six year old girl whom he would play with occasionally. Today she was sitting alone in a corner with a doll in her arms.

"Sherri's dad died in the accident," I explained in a whisper. He had been killed when the terrorists burst through the gate. We hadn't been able to save any of the medical personnel that were run down.

"You mean when we were attacked?" Kids seemed to get to the truth no matter how hard you tried to sugarcoat it. Too many 'accidents' claiming too many lives.

"Yes, honey. Sherri needs your help. She needs you to be extra nice to her and to help her through this hard time, okay?"

"Okay, but Blank Man is actually helping her right now."

Jesus, *Blank Man*. The name always upset me. I believed it was because of the letter Joel had left – his suicide letter which mentioned a *Blank Man* more than once in almost every stanza of his poem.

"*Blank Man* is here?"

"Yup. He's helping explain to her what happened."

"What's he saying to her, Leif?" I leaned into him and looked at the corner where Sherri sat moving the arms of her doll up and down, nodding her head.

"He's just explaining where her dad is now." Leif sat abruptly on the carpeted floor and picked up a toy.

"And where is *that*, Leif. Heaven?" A surge of excitement overcame me. I felt I was on the verge of learning the mysteries of life after death. Where do we go when we die?

"That's not what I meant, Mom. I meant he's telling her where he is in life."

"What does *that* mean?"

"He's in a *baby* now."

Reincarnation. Okay, I'd bite.

"His spirit is in a new body?" I asked.

"I guess so. I guess that's what that means." He knew more than he was telling me.

A question arose in my head like thunder and I asked it without the benefit of forethought. "Did the *Blank Man* tell you if you were someone else before you were you?"

"I was. So were you, so were *all* of us!' Leif became very animated, almost angry.

"Okay, honey. If that's what you believe..."

"That's the *truth*, Mom! We come and we go and we come and we go, it's kind of stupid when you think about it. Why keep coming back for? It's like going to school all your life!"

That was pretty profound for an eight year-old. If this was true, then the Hindus and the Buddhists had it right. We keep coming back to learn more and more and when we achieve enlightenment we stop coming back. I'd read an interesting book on the subject while at the bunker, with my witches. This begged the question I had been struggling with a very long time.

"Did he tell you *who* you were before you were you?" I asked again.

"Uh-huh." He moved a toy wagon up his left leg and down his right.

I asked because I'd been harboring a theory of my own that the witches hadn't even touched on. Though it was confirmed his was an *old* soul, *whose* soul was the real question. Leif's right forearm bore a distinctive mark, a birthmark that ran full around the circumference of it. It was a faint line that had actually gotten quite a bit darker in the past eight years. It was just below the elbow.

"He said I was *Joel*."

Chapter Forty-One

He was Joel, his *father*. Those words would haunt my every waking hour for many days to come. The idea that Joel had lived on in his own son floored me. Yes, I had been playing with the idea, having read in some occult book that occasionally a past life will represent itself in the body of a new life through markings. Old scars, old wounds that carried their energy across the - whatever it had to carry it across- dimensions? Joel's arm had been removed at exactly the point Leif's markings were appearing. The coincidence was too uncanny to even absorb.

Never mind the fact that the spirit, or angel, or whatever you wanted to call it was still with us, with him, still guiding him in some fashion. I sincerely worried for my son's life, for his future. Joel's angel had not missed a beat. He'd let Joel die, and then he reconnected. I needed answers.

"Sara." It was Sergeant Jones calling me from just beyond the entrance to the day care.

"Yes?" I answered blankly.

"Could I see you a moment?"

"Sure."

In the hallway he took me by the arm softly and positioned himself between me and the door. "Jimmy told me what happened up in the tower. I just wanted to thank you."

"Oh yeah, of course." I struggled to snap out of my most recent revelation.

"No, really. I couldn't bear the thought of my wife and kids without a father and a husband in all of this. Thank God for small miracles."

"I – I couldn't imagine this place without *you*." I felt the familiar heat building up in my face and chest.

"Thanks, Sara, really. I was lucky to have had you up there."

"I'm glad I could help." My voice cracked. His face was only inches away from mine. I could feel his breath on my lips. My eyelids fluttered, independent of my will.

"My guardian angel." He smiled widely.

I would have felt uncomfortable in the moment if I hadn't liked him so much. I half expected him to kiss me. God, I wished he had. But I knew my place, and accepted his heartfelt thanks. Though this back and forth had gone on for years with Sergeant Jones, I still found it difficult to navigate. In *life* a man, or boy as it were, would profess his lust for me within the first ten minutes of meeting me. I knew I carried off a certain look that others found attractive. With the Sergeant, though, and his situation, he couldn't, or wouldn't tell me that in so many words. So, the game played on.

"Let's hope that's the last of the raids," I added when I felt I had control over my voice again.

"I'm sure there are more to this terror cell then the ten we stumbled upon." He turned and looked down the narrow hallway. "I'd like to get to them before they come looking for our prisoner."

"You believe you've captured their leader?" I switched gears and began fishing for information on Earl.

"Yes, he's admitted as much. About all he *will* admit though. He's in the stockade now. We've been questioning him for days. He's a tough one to crack." He seemed frustrated.

"I could talk to him." I didn't think. I just spoke. "I mean, have you tried that approach, with a woman?"

"No." He shook his head. "You would be willing to talk to that animal?" His brow furrowed and eyes narrowed. The mole above his left eyebrow hid within the deep creases of his forehead.

"What do you need to know?"

"Well, whether there are more for one - where they might be hiding out. Their numbers, things like that."

"I could give it a shot."

"If you're sure, I'll set it up."

"I'm sure. Whatever I can do. This place saved my life and my son's life. There isn't *anything* I wouldn't do to help." It was true, but at the same time I found myself excited at the prospect of seeing Earl in captivity.

"You're a good soldier, Sara."

"Thanks." I blushed. My knees wobbled slightly and I discreetly held onto the door frame to steady myself. I was often embarrassed by my inability to control my reaction to his presence.

"I'll contact you in the morning and let you know. If you'd like I can be there, in the room while you interview him."

"Maybe. I'll think about it."

He left me there with a smile and a nod. Back to his wife and kids. I was sure I'd given myself away this time. Shake it off, Sara I told myself, and walked back into the day care.

Chapter Forty-Two

S ergeant Jones set it up. I was to come face-to-face with Earl. I would confront him alone. No need for the Sergeant to know I'd ever had anything to do with this asshole. Our interrogation was scheduled for the morning. After a restless night in my bunk where I ran through all of the things I'd say, I felt I was ready. The Sergeant picked me up at my room after I left Leif at day care.

"You're still good with this?" he asked as we walked the halls.

"I am." How would he react to seeing me? Although eight years had passed, I hadn't really changed.

We walked across the compound and entered the stockade where Earl was sitting on a cot in a cell. I took great pleasure in seeing him caged.

"Prisoner!" shouted Jeffrey. "It's time!"

Earl did not acknowledge us. The Sergeant looked at me and whispered into my ear. His hot breath tickled the flesh of my neck. "Would you like me to remain here?"

"No. If he hasn't told you anything yet, he won't talk for me if you're here."

"Be careful. He's very unstable."

"I'll be fine. He's in a cage. He can't hurt me." I whispered back.

"Very well. There's a pad and pen here if you feel the need to write anything down. Remember what we're looking for: numbers, location, strengths, weaknesses."

"I've got it, thanks." With that he left me in the small room. It smelled of sweat and blood. The room itself was little more than a closet. I sat down on the wooden chair and picked up the pen and pad.

Earl shifted in his cell; he was visibly uncomfortable. He had put up quite a fight when they took him, and no doubt his swollen cheek and closed eye were the result. It was especially strange to see him, someone from my past, like this. He was a grown man, no longer the untamable teenager. With so many of my friends from the past gone, I often wondered what they would look like when I studied my reflection. Now here was Earl, eight years older. The others would remain forever young in my memory. Joel, Caroline, the whole group. I was thankful for having had the opportunity to grow as a person, to grow up at all.

"Hello, Earl," I said. This got his attention. No one had been able to get a word out of him, let alone his name. He squinted at me.

"You *know* me? You know my *name*?"

"Look at me, and tell me you don't know me." I would enjoy this moment.

He looked up and then sideways, his face permanently etched with the reminder of the fire he'd survived. The fire I'd set. His left eye swollen shut from a more recent injury.

"*You*," he growled.

"Surprised?" I asked, with every bit of pride I could muster, sitting up straight.

"Sara," he said, his voice trailing. "How the *fuck* did you manage to get yourself to this place?"

"Ha! I could ask the same of you. I never would have guessed you've been the one sneaking around like an animal, causing us so much grief." I leaned closer to the bars. He leaped, salivating, but was restrained by a chain that held his wrists and ankles to the far wall. He let out a shriek, jerking back to the cot. My heart jumped out of my mouth despite my earlier confidence.

"Murderer!" he shouted. "You *bitch*! You fucking *murdering* bitch!"

The door to the building opened a crack and I waved the guard off.

I'd made peace with myself over what I'd done. I'd never regretted it, and I never would. Earl and his cronies, Fred and Kevin, had raped Caroline and executed Seth.

"Does it still hurt?" I asked him, tracing my fingers along the side of my face. The burn was a horrible scar to look at. "Has it hurt all these years? God I hope so."

"You fucking bitch…" That was all he could muster. I was almost happier knowing that he had survived all this time, suffering daily for his cruelty. "You *fucking* bitch…." He was quieting down now.

"You don't need to tell me anything, Earl. I don't give a shit about your ragtag little band of terrorists."

"Is that what they call us? Terrorists?" He seemed offended, shifting around on his cot, rattling his chains.

"Of course. You could have approached the base and asked for salvation, but you, the pig-headed, arrogant prick that you are, thought you could have it all."

"You don't know what you're talking about."

"I know *you*, Earl. That's all I need to know."

"You know *shit*." Drool ran from a split in his lip, touching his knee before it left his mouth. "What do you know? I've been a leader. I've managed to build an *Empire*!"

"You've managed to find yourself *here*. Like the criminal you are." Leaning in again, I whispered, "You know you'll die here, don't you?"

"I am the leader of *many*. I have many people answering to me."

"You have *shit*. What did you do? Hide in the woods? That's not leadership. That's being an animal. Hiding from civilization, taking what you need from others. You're no better than a dumb animal. You're the emperor of nothing!" I forced a laugh to further taunt him.

"What do you know? I have an *army* waiting for me."

"Hiding naked in the trees no doubt, waiting for their *emperor* to return with some scraps." I could see he had become increasingly agitated by my comments. Perhaps I would get information from him after all.

"We are not animals! We have it better than we did with *Joel*. We live in a castle!" He stared at me through the iron bars, his one good eye trained on me. "A *castle*!"

I had learned the local geography during my eight years here. There was only one place I knew that was ever called a castle. It was the Castle Peaks, the rough survey of rock that jutted up into the horizon some three hundred feet. When the sun set in the west, the resulting silhouette would form the illusion of a castle on a ridge.

I stood up and smiled. "The Castle Peaks, Earl?" His face collapsed and any color that might have been present faded to white. "Is *that* where we should go?" I studied his reaction.

"I don't know where that is," he said automatically, crossing his arms in front of him. "I don't know where that is."

"I think you *do,* Earl. I think that's where your little hideout is and I think I'll let the Sergeant know so he can take the soldiers there and bomb the living *shit* out of it." I knew the Sergeant would approach those frightened and demoralized people with a solution rather than firepower, but for this purpose, I needed Earl to believe they would use force. "You've just become your own worst enemy. And now, not only will *you* die a wretched soulless piece of garbage, all your little accomplices will too."

Earl studied his hands, clenching his fists. Snapping sounds echoed off the bars from his knuckles. He would repeat this over and over. "You know," he began very solemnly, "Seth *begged* for his life. Before I had Kevin gag him. He kicked and kicked in his noose until he strangled to death. I thought it fitting. Just like his buddy, Gil. And then there were Caroline and Sid, I came upon them in the backyard, having escaped your little Barbeque."

He was trying to hurt me now. A last ditch effort to come out on top. But I had always wondered who had murdered Caroline and Sid, and so, morbidly I listened.

"Caroline was coughing from the smoke while Sid tried to wave it away from her face. I watched them kneel down, behind the pool house and realized the fire was no accident, that you three had planned it. They were outfitted with heavy bags full of provisions and hauling the four gallon containers of water. I waited for you to show up so I could take you all down at once. But when you didn't, I decided to ask them myself where I could find you."

My eyes burned as I listened, remembering the night, the explosion, my friends.

"I was able to catch them by surprise. Caroline stuttered something and Sid was so confused. *'Surprise!'* I said and shot the pistol out of his hand. Then I turned the gun on Caroline and asked where you were. *'Where is she? Where is that bitch?'* I asked. Sid tried to jump me but I put him down with one shot. Then Caroline jabbed her knife into my foot and I shot her." He laughed callously. "That foot never really healed right." He showed it to me, lifting the heavy chains.

"You're *garbage,* Earl." My chin trembled, my face soaked in tears. I wiped them away with both palms, sucking in a deep breath.

"Maybe," he allowed, lowering his foot. "But I am a survivor, like you. I took what I could carry from them, and made my way to the barn garden where I camped out for months, hoping one day you would show up, so I could finish you off."

"But I didn't," I said defiantly.

"No, you didn't." He seemed almost respectful with that statement. "And what happened to that baby of yours?"

"Never mind my baby."

"Come on, we're just catching up here."

"Fuck you, Earl." I stood.

"So, you'll tell your Sergeant about my hideout and then what?"

"*You'll* hang."

"I suppose I will." His head bobbed up and down. Something about him had changed over the course of our conversation. He seemed somehow more relaxed, more in control of himself. I wanted him panicked, afraid of his fate.

"You'll hang as an example. But no one will come to your funeral. Your body will be burned to ashes. No one will avenge your death, no one will care. You will not be martyred. You will only cease to exist." I walked to the door and knocked for the guard. "You go to hell, Earl, and you *stay* there."

Chapter Forty-Three

The operation went off without a hitch. The soldiers stormed the hideout of Castle Peak. A few men were shot in the assault. But when they entered the rocky cavern, they found a community of women and children.

"They were frightened, but glad to see us all the same," Sergeant Jones remarked as we sat in the mess hall the night of the raid, chewing on a stick of meat that had been dried and stored in one of the underground lockers years before. "They're in the hospital now, with their children."

"I heard. I'm supposed to help tomorrow with the dental exams. That's incredible. How many were there?"

"Eight women, ranging in age from seventeen to forty-five, but we'll gather that information along with their names, where they originated and how long they'd lived at Castle Peak."

"And the children?" I felt awful for the children. I thought of Leif living under Earl's rule, in that place, and it made me sad.

"Some seventeen kids, from newborns right up to six years old. They were living like animals, their clothes rags. And the dysentery. *Jesus*. They were dehydrated as well. I think that's what pushed Earl to make this last stand against us." He paused to drink from his cup. "It's a good thing you did in there. You got exactly what we needed from him. You're a good soldier."

I loved it when he called me that. "I'm here to serve," I said, sending him a weak salute.

"It's incredible that you knew him too. That you *lived* in that house with him and your friends. That's *unbelievable*." He meant it too; it *was* pretty unbelievable, after eight years, that Earl had taken the same direction I had, at least physically. Of course, our lives could not have ended up more differently.

"There's lots more to that story I haven't told you, but now that he's here, I'd like to volunteer more information. More crimes he committed against my friends, which he's never answered for."

"He'll hang for what he's done regardless. But if it will bring you peace, we'll hear it at his trial."

We rose and left to go our separate ways, him to his wife and kids, and I to the daycare to pick up Leif. The children were practicing a play for the coming holidays. It was nice to celebrate the holidays again. All that time at Joel's house, we'd celebrated just one birthday. God, it seemed like several lifetimes ago. Funny, that thought brought back what Leif had said about reincarnation. What if hanging Earl wasn't the end of Earl?

"Sara!" It was Jess, a girl from the daycare staff. She was waving at me from across the compound while running in my direction. "Sara!!"

"Yes, Jess? What's up?"

"It's Leif, Sara."

My heart stopped. "What about Leif?" I felt a distinctive pain in my chest and my left arm began to tingle. If anything happened to Leif, *I would not survive*, I knew this.

"He's missing."

Chapter Forty-Four

Where was my son?! The *Blank Man* was to blame for this. Or the angel, or whatever it was. That omnipotent presence which had embedded itself into my life like a tick, preaching destiny to my boyfriend, and now, to his son. What if Leif's destiny had him running away from here, from me? Panic rising, I gathered myself up and ran towards the daycare, Jess hot on my heals. I was trying to rationalize where Leif could be. Could he have wandered off on his own? It wasn't like him, and this certainty was causing my anxiety to grow exponentially.

I stopped Jess at the door to the day care to catch my breath and turned her to face me. Her eyes were red and teary.

"Don't blame yourself, Jess. He's somewhere. We'll find him." I didn't want her burdened by guilt. I needed her to be sharp, to remember everything. She nodded and smiled.

"I need you to tell me exactly what he was doing and where he was situated in the room the last time you saw him." She nodded again and we moved into the daycare. It was empty now. The rehearsal had ended and the group disbanded. I scanned the room for Leif's favorite toys.

Jess pointed toward a corner next to a toy chest. "That's the last place I saw him. He was sitting on the chest and playing with a toy, talking to it."

"Okay, good. Do you remember what time that was?"

"It must have been just after seven, Sara. We had finished a snack for break, so it must have been 7:15."

I walked to the corner and picked up a doll. It was a soldier doll, twelve inches tall. I studied it for a moment. "And you checked my room, and the washrooms?" I asked her.

"I checked everywhere I could think to check before I found you."

"We need to announce this to the base." I said. "I'm going to call the Sergeant." I picked up the intercom and dialed Sergeant Jones's room number. When he answered I quickly told him what I knew.

"I'll send an announcement to the base. We can mobilize a search party right away. Sara, it'll be okay, we'll find him tonight. He's probably just hiding somewhere."

"Thanks. Thank you." I was becoming frantic, I could sense it. My resolve was starting to crack.

"Sara, meet me at the hospital. We'll start there."

I hung up and went to my room for a final check. I was hoping I'd see him sitting on his bed, waiting for me to take him for a bath or change into his pajamas. He was not there.

"CODE AMBER. SEARCH PARTIES FORM IN THE COMPOUND. REPEAT CODE AMBER." The base had several codes for search parties, and several search parties designated to each code. In the case of a "*code amber*", everyone was involved.

Chapter Forty-Five

What felt like hours took no more than twenty minutes. The search groups were designated to specific sites. My group searched the perimeter in case Leif had found a way out. My eyes focused on every inch of ground as we followed the fence line, looking for something he may have dropped, some escape route he may have invented. All I saw was dirt, dry and dusty.

Finally, the soldier in charge of our crew heard a crackling sound on his walkie-talkie. I rushed forward to hear the news, full of dread. "We've found him."

"Roger that."

I waited.

"He's in the stockade." The stockade? "We will reunite him with his mother at the hospital." With that I set off running.

He had been found by one of the soldiers in what should have been a locked stockade, sitting opposite Earl. They told me he was unharmed. Although he had not a scratch on him, I knew Earl, and I knew he had more than one way to hurt a person. They had not been able to get an answer out of Leif as to how he had ended up there.

After we were reunited, Leif and I went to the showers where I washed and dried him and took him to bed. I was silent the whole time. He knew he had done something very wrong. I was fighting back tears of joy, but also anger. Why had he gone to see Earl?

In our room I asked these questions after tucking him in.

"It was Blank Man. He showed me where to go, where the key was hidden and…"

"You do everything the *Blank Man* says?"

"Mostly." He shrugged, as though the question were somehow silly.

"What have I told you about the *Blank Man*? Haven't I made myself clear? You do what *I* say, and tell me everything *he* says."

"He's not trying to hurt us, Mom."

"Oh, really? Having you break into the stockade and then hold a conversation with a dangerous prisoner isn't trying to hurt you?"

"He is in *jail*, Mom. He couldn't hurt me." His head pushed further into his pillow as he became more uncomfortable with the conversation. "He said he knew Daddy."

Goddamn that Earl. "How does he know who *you* are?" I asked. "Did you tell him I was your mother?"

"That's the first thing he asked when I got there."

"So you told him."

"Uh huh."

"What else did you tell him?"

"I don't know. I didn't really do much talking."

"What did *he* talk about?" I felt a sudden chill and rubbed my arms as I sat at Leif's bedside.

"He said you were all friends."

"I was *never* Earl's friend, Leif. We all lived together before you were born, but I was never his *friend.*"

"He said you were. He said he saw Daddy in me. That I had his eyes and his nose."

"That's true: your daddy was a very handsome man. And so are you. And you're smart too."

"Like you, Mom?"

"Sure Leif, like me."

"That's what he said, that you were a very smart lady." A compliment from Earl. That seemed unlikely, but Leif had no reason to lie to me.

"I still don't understand why the *Blank Man* sent you to see *him.*"

"He said I should know my enemy." My spine tingled.

"Did your *Blank Man* tell you why *Earl* was your enemy?"

"No, he just said *I should know my enemy* and then took me to the jail."

"Well, you don't have to worry about Earl becoming your enemy. In a few days he won't be able to hurt anyone ever again."

"That's not what Blank Man told me."

"Go to sleep, Leif. Sweet dreams, and remember, I love you."

"I love you too, Mom."

Leif fell into a deep sleep while I remained wide awake, wishing away the *Blank Man*. I watched his chest rise and fall, grateful he'd been returned to me unharmed. But the crazy circumstances that had taken him from me in the first place baffled me. Could I really believe in *Blank Man*? Was this spirit trying to harm my son? Were my witches wrong? Just as these thoughts circled through my head, I saw him. A shadowy figure materialized at the end of Leif's bed.

Chapter Forty-Six

I knew it was him. There was no face, just a form. And as quickly as it appeared, it vanished. Still I knew this was it. The same apparition that had caused so much heartache for myself and my friends so long ago. And now was controlling my son, guiding him right into the arms of my enemy. *"Know your enemy"* it had told Leif, but Earl was *my* enemy, not Leif's. Besides, Earl would be hanged in just a few short days. Then I remembered the words that had been passed on to me through Leif. *"We all come back."* A shiver overtook me at the memory. To think Earl might reemerge as some unsuspecting mother's newborn made my blood run cold.

Something more began to work its way into my head as the thought evolved. What if I was interpreting this the wrong way? What if he escaped from his cell? What if he reestablished an army and came back? I couldn't imagine that in his weakened condition he would have any hope of breaking free. So why did this thought continue to haunt me?

Checking once more to confirm that my son was asleep, I left the room, locking the door behind me. I found myself walking in the direction of the hospital. What if the women and children we'd taken in actually felt some twisted affection towards their captor? What if one or all of them decided to free Earl? Jesus, that was a concern. My pace picked up, and I began running across the compound towards the hospital. The clouds were gathering overhead, grey and black. It would rain very soon.

When I reached the hospital I threw open the doors and they crashed against the walls. The refugees were startled, as were the doctor and nurses. I scanned the large room and performed a head count.

"Sorry," I apologized. "Is everyone here?"

"What do you mean, Sara?" The doctor approached me from his desk.

"The refugees," I answered. "Are they all accounted for?"

"Yes, I believe so. Sonja, could we have a headcount please?" Sonja nodded.

"What's this about, Sara?" He looked concerned. I rubbed at my arms. It was a cool night, and with the promise of rain I felt a chill rise in me.

"Just a hunch, Doctor."

"Everyone is accounted for," called Sonja. A wave of relief. I would have to talk to the Sergeant about my concern. "All but one," Sonja finished. My heart fell.

Shit. It would only take one. "Shit." I said.

"Sara, what's going on?" The doctor stood, placing his clipboard on his desk.

"Just a hunch," I repeated on my way out.

As I began moving toward the soldiers' barracks I stopped and turned to face the jail. What if I could stop it from happening? I decided to visit the jail first.

I entered the building, which was deserted this time of night. The one bulb that remained lit in the hallway provided barely enough light. But I could see all I needed to. The door was ajar. My heart stopped. My right hand swung up to soothe a searing pain, rubbing it away. The light above the door flickered, yellow. I looked out to see the windmills turning frantically against the wind. The scene seemed apocalyptic. If Earl was loose in the base, we were in real trouble.

Chapter Forty-Seven

E arl was gone. He'd been freed by one of the refugees. I explained this to the Sergeant, wrapped in a heavy blanket, my son at my side. "I'm certain of it." I continued. "They're missing one of the women from the hospital, a woman without a child. She's likely so brainwashed that she's gone and broken him out."

"We've got the perimeter under full guard now, Sara. If he's still inside the base, we'll flush him out." He walked to the window, staring out blankly. "This is our *fault*. We should have had a guard on him. And the refugees, they seemed so relieved to have been rescued."

"Don't blame yourself, Jeff," I didn't like seeing him like this. "Honestly, I'm afraid this is all my fault."

"*Your* fault, how so?"

"He gave it up too easily. The information about their hideout. He also knew we would bring the women and children back. He knew we might kill off the rest of the men in a shootout, but the women and children... he knew we'd bring them back."

"You think he gave up his camp just on the chance that one of them would free him?"

"Knowing Earl, yes." My head dropped, and Leif gently rubbed my back. "He is very clever, and the fact that he has no conscience makes choices like that easy for him. He played the odds and he played me, and it looks as though he's won."

"He hasn't won the war, Sara. He's only won a battle."

"Still, he's loose now." I looked at Leif, whose little forehead was wrinkled, his eyes big and sad.

*****

In our room I put Leif back to bed. It was very late, and he needed to sleep. I changed and got into my own cot. Turning on my side, my back to Leif, I started to cry. Why does this *Blank Man* not *do* something? What's the purpose of a higher intelligence if all they're capable of doing is guiding a person in the wrong direction? Why let someone like Earl continue to plague us? Part of the grand plan? Fuck the grand plan!

I felt a hand on my exposed shoulder and an arm wrap itself around me. "Don't be sad, Mommy." Leif crawled under my covers and settled behind me, hugging me. My hand reached up to touch his. "Everything will be okay." I wondered if he actually knew that, or if he was just comforting me in the moment.

"Thank you, Leif. I love you."

"I love you too. Please don't be sad." His logic, that I could stop being sad just because he wanted me to struck me as profound. I turned and lay on my back. He was right. There was nothing I could do except love my son, no matter what happened. I kissed his forehead. Leif adjusted and we fell asleep.

*****

I awoke with a start. My eyes flew to the clock over Leif's bed. 3:33 am. I shifted, slowly sitting up so as not to wake Leif. I sat on the edge of the cot and rubbed my eyes. Whenever I woke up prematurely like this, there was not much chance I was going to get back to sleep. This was when my mind would relive the horrors of my past. Images I couldn't escape ran over and over again in my head. The scenarios I'd lived through would haunt me, and tonight was no different. Feeling sick, I stood up, paced a moment and then lay down on Leif's bed. I breathed in deeply for four seconds, held for seven, then released over eight and repeated. Sometimes this rhythmic breathing left me dizzy, but almost always left me feeling better.

I sat up and crossed my legs. Eyes still closed, I straightened my back and pushed my chest out, rolling my neck. Opening my eyes I was confronted once again by an image I had fought so hard against believing. Sitting not two feet in front of me, cross-legged as best as I could tell, was *Blank Man*. He was very dark, a silhouette. I froze.

A sound very weak rose in my head. Someone was speaking at a distance. It became clearer the longer I stared back at the Blank Man. It was *him*. He was trying to communicate with me. His head cocked to the left and suddenly the words became very clear.

"Ask your questions." He was soft-spoken, and I had to strain to hear, but inherently I understood. I felt the hairs on my arms rise with goose bumps. This was my chance, I thought. This was the opportunity I'd been waiting for.

"Ask your questions," he repeated. What *were* my questions? I drew a blank. Oh shit, I was going to blow this. He must have sensed my anxiety. He placed a hand on my knee. It felt like nothing. Not cold, not warm, not there. The act calmed me though, and I was able to remember the questions I had wanted to ask.

First I asked a question I'd wanted answered when Leif first brought up the Blank Man. "Are you Joel's angel? *Our* angel?"

"Yes," he answered. His voice was soft. I guessed I'd always known that, but was relieved to know I was right.

The next question was broader and I hoped I'd get a more detailed answer. This was something I wanted Joel to ask his angel for me but never got around to putting it to him. "Why us? Why now? How is it *we* are the generation that has to live through the end of the world?"

The Blank Man's head cocked to the right. "*We?* You say that as though you are separating yourself from those that have come before you. *We* all come back. *You* have lived before, as your son has lived through Joel. You have lived through another, and another and another. You are experiencing this time as you experienced the Black Plague, the Second World War, the Inquisition. You have lived before as surely as you will live again to experience again and again. You are here now because you are an important means to this end. Leif is here now because he *is* that end."

Reincarnation. He was talking about reincarnation. *We all come back* was what he'd told Leif when he explained to him that he was Joel, his *father*. "Why would Joel die and be replaced by Leif? Couldn't Joel have done what Leif is destined to do?"

"Joel had lost what ability he had left in him to lead. His addiction had taken over."

"Did Joel have anything to do with Connor's death?" I realized I wasn't speaking but rather only thinking my questions now. "No, don't answer that," I said out loud. I was better off not knowing, I'd decided.

"What is Leif destined to do?"

"This is yet unclear."

"Unclear? How could it be unclear? Isn't destiny clarity by definition?"

"This is why we have such an interest in Leif, and why we held such interest in Joel. Destiny is not absolute. It is driven by fate."

"What's the difference?"

"Consider fate as an outside entity acting through a person, while destiny is brought about by the person themself. Both march towards a predetermined end, but how they get there can affect that end."

"Are you that outside entity?"

"I am only a guide."

Questions started jumping into my head. I felt an urgency to ask them all before he disappeared. "Why allow Earl to escape? Why has he not yet been punished for all he's done?"

"Earl too has a part to play, and fate has seen fit to allow this course to unveil itself in time."

"I don't understand. Who's running this show?"

"Show?"

"Yes. Life. What is it all for?"

"Life is a *lesson*. When it is learned, only then will you understand what it was all for."

"So, who's right? Christians? Buddhists? Islam...."

"Religion is a beginning. It was meant to be the teacher."

"But we messed that up didn't we?"

"Religion became a means to rule rather than teach."

"Why are you telling me all of this now?"

"Leif is a special boy. Protect him, keep him safe and I will guide him as best as I can."

"Better than you led Joel?"

"Joel had his own ideas. He fought me and he fought his destiny. I could not alter his path towards self destruction. He was filled with anger in the end, guilt, hate, frustration. It would be difficult to say whether he could have recovered enough to become leader in what must come to pass. With Leif, we start anew, and you can help. We can work together in this."

With that, Blank Man disintegrated before my eyes, black spots dancing on my eyeballs. I lay back and covered my mouth with my hands, staring up at the ceiling. "Holy shit."

Chapter Forty-Eight

E arl and his woman friend were never found. During the days that followed his escape, the soldiers hunted the surrounding area and placed men at the Castle Rock in case he returned, but he was never seen again. The Sergeant and I questioned the refugees from Earl's camp. Where might they have gone? What might they do next? They were all very forthcoming but for the most part none of them could answer our questions with any certainty. One interesting fact came from a conversation with the oldest of the women, Sybil, who had three young children from three different men. She said that Earl himself had not fathered any of the children.

"He blamed me, but when you force yourself on so many women and still, no children, you need to take a closer look at yourself."

"He's always thought of himself as the Alpha male." I responded. I had a flashback to the time I stumbled upon his journal. He spoke of destroying the homosexuals, and those unable (or unwilling) to have children. He saw repopulating the planet as every person's duty. Yet here he had proven he could not have children of his own.

The woman who had freed Earl had been young, and probably quite taken with her leader. Just seventeen, Mary blindly followed him in everything. Earl would have thought he'd have his best chance to conceive with the youngest of them, and so kept Mary in his own tent. His control over her had led to his escape, and so the most I could hope, is that we never saw him again.

*****

I took Leif to the greenhouse the day following my encounter with Blank Man. Leif had taken an interest in nature, and studied one plant in particular. He would go daily to watch this plant develop from a seedling to a towering tree. With each new development his amazement never ceased to amuse me. But on this day, I brought him there hoping we could talk. The greenhouse was humid inside, no matter what the season. The smell of pine permeated the place, washing away the distinctively chemical smell of the outdoors. Next to the barn animals, this place most inspired him. We walked through the aisles, pine needles and dried leaves from the fruit trees that lined the concrete floor pad crunching underfoot.

The army Chaplain, and our full time botanist, was a tall man of African descent. He wore army issue glasses, a buzz cut and always dressed with his collar exposed, making him readily recognizable as a man of the cloth. We'd shared a few brief conversations over the course of my occupancy at the base.

The saplings had taken off during the last six years, and upon entering the greenhouse one was reminded of the indigenous forests that once populated the local landscape. The man-made ponds that acted as fisheries bred trout, bass and also feeder fish like minnows. The idea was that the Chaplain and his team would tag the fish and place them in Elle Lake, which was a mere stone's throw from the base. This process was repeated time and again in a netted area roughly ten thousand square feet along the lake's southern shores. This area was under heavy guard to prevent poaching. The objective was to have the fish repopulate the lifeless lake. The experiment worked, as the fish adjusted quickly to the lake water, feeding off the abundant fly population that bred along the shores in the dead fish the Chaplain's team had placed for that very reason.

We found the Chaplain at one of the fish ponds, where Leif snatched up a shell from the rock wall.

"What are these?" I asked, pulling it from Leif's hand.

"Zebra mussels," the Chaplain replied. "They multiply like rabbits and eat all the toxins out of a fresh water lake. They number in the thousands in Elle Lake now, feeding along the lake bed, scooping up all the nasty goo that has collected there, suffocating the soil." He knelt down beside Leif as he explained the process, his palms clapping together as he demonstrated the mussels at work. Leif got a kick out of it.

"Sounds cool." Leif was truly fascinated.

"I'm excited about it," he agreed and stood up, patting Leif lightly on his head. "We're also considering planting a few of the hardier pines next month beyond the family housing buildings and maybe even the apple trees."

"Wow," I mused. "You were *really* prepared for the worst weren't you?" I shook my head in awe of the planning that would have gone into this place. Hundreds of indigenous seeds stored, hundreds of plants in seedling form, fish eggs, animals to breed, birds of a dozen different varieties, a bee hive. There wasn't much they'd missed. This base was like Noah's ark.

"It's a testament to man's understanding of his environment. Of course, if the earth rejects our efforts, it was all for not."

"Are you nervous about the planting?"

"Yes, of course, but I am also very encouraged. I believe life will find its footing again." He pointed down to where an ant hill had formed in a crack in the cement. "Look at that. Have you ever seen an ant, Leif?" he asked kneeling down again with my son for a closer look, careful not to disturb the colony.

"I've seen pictures," Leif said, bright-eyed. "Look at them all, Mom. Look."

I knelt down beside him. "Aren't they amazing, Leif? Did you know they can lift 10 times their own body weight?"

"Ten times! Wow." He was mesmerized by their movements. Each step taken with a clear purpose of survival.

"I've been feeding them since I first discovered the colony," he admitted, smiling ear to ear. "This is just another example of life reclaiming what it had temporarily lost. God's creatures. Resilient, aren't we?"

I smiled tight-lipped up at him and stood. "You must have a pretty interesting opinion on what's happened, Chaplain."

"Must I?"

"Mustn't you? Isn't *this* the end time? Haven't we been living through the Apocalypse these past nine years?"

"As a man of God, I can say with conviction that the end of the age was prophesized. And an ending of sorts did occur."

"And what about Jesus?"

"What about Him?" He moved to the raised pond and shook a can of fish food over the water.

"Well, I guess what I mean is, where *is* He?"

"You're referring to the Second Coming." His tone became tighter, like he'd been asked the question a thousand times. I moved closer to him while Leif remained behind, fascinated by the six legged insects.

"That's the *big* one, isn't it? *Where is He?*" He placed the fish food down, picked up a towel, wiped his hands and turned to face me. "Why hasn't He come to rebuild His kingdom? When will the thousand years of peace begin?"

"Exactly."

"I'll tell you what I've told those that attend my sermons. That I can only quote the Bible, Sara, I do not presume to understand God's plan, only to have faith in His divine will."

"No offence, Chaplain, but, isn't that a bit of a cop-out?" I flicked at the water abruptly with my fingers, frightening the dozens of fish into the far corner.

"Faith is a paradoxical thing isn't it, Sara? You suffer an experience, or a vision, or a miracle, however you'd like to categorize it, and you find faith. Look at me. I was a botanist for many years before I was called into the service of the Lord. I studied plants, right down to the atomic level, and do you know what I found?"

"No."

"God, Sara. I found God in those perfect, intelligently designed life forms. And imagine, if I could find God in a plant, God must be everywhere, in everything. I was blessed with new vision, to see God in *all* things. But just because *my* faith was secured, doesn't make it make sense to someone else. We all must experience our own epiphany."

I shifted my weight from one leg to the other. "I understand faith. I do. But Revelations spoke of this time, did it not? *Isn't* this the end?"

His bottom lip curled. "I guess not." He walked past me toward the vegetable garden and I followed, warning Leif not to move from his current fixation.

"So why destroy the earth if you're not going to start anew?"

"I'm not saying an ending didn't occur. But as for Armageddon... well, how could it be? Jesus has not revealed Himself to us." He turned again to address me. "According to Scripture, a great battle between good and evil must still take place. From what we know, evil struck the planet nine years ago. Perhaps in those nine years Satan has been recruiting his army while God has been preparing His."

"You think there will be more?" I shuddered at the thought. "You think *this* hasn't been enough?" I was becoming visibly shaken. "Chaplain, how much *more* can we take?"

"God gives us strength, Sara. Take comfort in that, and in your son."
He'd noticed my composure had taken a turn. His hands on my shoulders felt reassuring, but nothing would remove the fear I felt in *another* end,

worse than the one we'd just lived through, *were* living through. My faith in something greater, something that was leading us to some kind of salvation was shaken to the core.

Chapter Forty-Nine

Ten days after my discussion with the Chaplain at the greenhouse, I walked through the halls en route to the mess hall. I was late to meet Leif for a movie.

The hall was sparsely populated with late afternoon movie goers and filled with the aroma of pop corn. I noticed that the feature would begin shortly as I scanned the building for my son.

Having spotted him I walked to where Leif was standing, staring out the window at the rain as it punched into the earth, his palms flat against the glass and his forehead pressed against the back of his hands. The rains had been relentless for three days and didn't show any signs of retreat. Leif was becoming despondent, aching to go outdoors. Any drawn-out duration of rain like that sent my heart plummeting to my stomach, reminding me of the first few months after the bombs fell. Sometimes I wondered how any of us survived it: that claustrophobic feeling you get when you feel caged in, the sameness of the day to day, same people, same problems, same solutions. Gil hadn't survived it. I forced the memories from my head and focused again on Leif.

To think that my son would ever have to know such sadness produced a lump in my throat. Still, those days were behind me. I had every confidence the sun would shine again as it had after every heavy storm during the past nine years. I put a hand on Leif's shoulder and squeezed. He tore his gaze away from the window and looked up at me. I offered a comforting smile and he returned the gesture.

"It won't last forever, Leif," I assured him.

"I know, but I want to kick the ball around." His face sank.

I knelt down in front of him and he turned to face me. "Hey, why don't we use this time to do something together, just you and me?" I suggested.

"Like what?"

"Well, we could play a game." My mind raced to think of ways to entertain him. Then something pinched my leg in my jean pocket. Remembering the contents - I realized it offered the perfect solution. "For instance, have you ever played the game… pendulum?"

"Pendulum?" He'd probably never heard the word before. I inched the delicate silver chain from my pocket and let the heavy ring threaded through the chain fall from my palm. The chain fell taut, stopping eight inches from my hand, wrapped around my index finger.

Leif's little hands reached for the pendulum, a gift from my witches. It was one of my prized possessions, bringing me back to that feeling of having some control over my own destiny. He rubbed the silver chain carefully between his thumb and forefingers, moving down to the ring that dangled at the end.

"This is a pen-du-lum?" he asked, still transfixed by the shiny metal.

"Yup, well, it's a kind of pendulum."

"What does it do?"

"It can answer questions." This seemed like the easiest way to give Leif a sense of what would be asked of him in the future. If he felt he could control something like this with his mind, maybe he would believe that in all things.

I watched as confusion entered his eyes, forcing up his thick eyebrows.

"Well, I mean, it can't *talk*, but it can answer questions if you ask them." I had piqued his interest. When I situated myself on the tile floor, Leif followed suit. We were seated cross legged, facing each other with the storm outside as our backdrop. I held the chain up and offered it to him. "Take it and hold it as I am holding it."

Leif gently removed the chain from around my finger and wrapped it once around his own.

"Good, Leif," I congratulated. "Now, hold it out in front of you…"

I continued to explain how he could make the pendulum swing at will and to decide a circular motion meant *yes* and back and forth meant *no*. Then I had him ask yes or no questions, some about things he knew the answers to and others he would like to know the answers to. We sat there for more than two hours while the movie played, all the while Leif learning about the abilities he never knew he had. Waiting to be found, and used.

Chapter Fifty

From our first "lesson" in the mess hall, Leif's curiosity about all things paranormal seemed to explode. He became hungry for knowledge and I only hoped our library at the base had something to offer Leif in his quest.

"You can access the digital files if you can't find what you're looking for in paperback," the librarian reminded us. Tina was a short woman with an olive complexion who had once lived north of the base. She had told us that the collapse of her hometown had been vicious. While not directly hit by nuclear missiles, the city imploded about a week after the toxic clouds arrived. Riots, gang wars, police brutality, everything you saw on the news in *life* when a city suffered a black-out in their poorest sector was experienced tenfold city-wide when the public realized that they were never going to recover.

Tina's duties in the library were far greater than organizing the books. She also kept records for the base: a day to day journal of all operations, including people entering and exiting. Hers was a position I found very intriguing. She was writing a new history. She used the Gregorian calendar, but also, secretly, began a new calendar beginning at year *1* from the date the bombs fell. She called it AA – After the Apocalypse. So, we were nine years into this calendar, 9AA.

"Can you look up Buddhism for me? Leif is really interested in reincarnation and stuff like that," I said, never alluding to his true interest. I didn't want anyone to think Leif was born for some great role. As long as he knew it, and I knew it, that was enough.

"Oh, we have some paperbacks on that subject, Sara. Last row, numbers 500 through 510."

"Perfect, thanks, Tina." The library wasn't big, but it was certainly a treat to have. I'd read much of what it had to offer. I had checked out a few books from the digital archives, but those you had to read in the library at one of the three computer stations.

I found the book I thought would most intrigue Leif and checked it out. Tina gave me a distracted smile on my way through.

"Goodnight, Tina."

"Mmhmm," she managed, typing frantically into her laptop.

On my way back through the barracks, I ran into the Sergeant just outside the family housing buildings. My heart fluttered and I felt the familiar heat escaping through my cheeks.

"Oh, Sara," he said as he saw me approach. "What a coincidence, I was just thinking about you."

The corners of my mouth immediately reached skyward, parting my lips in a ridiculous grin. I must have always seemed awkward to him. The game had gone on for so long. I didn't know how to end it.

"Hi, Jeff," I greeted in a high-pitched squeak. He grinned back at me, always in control.

"Sara." His hand touched my upper arm, closing gently, guiding me into him until we were inches away from each other.

"What's up?" Our eyes met and I quickly looked down at my book.

"I wanted to talk to you about something." His eyebrows pulled together as I snuck another look at his face. "Huh," he continued. "I completely forgot what I was about to say."

"Oh, well. Whatever it was will come back to you." I smiled shyly.

He shook his head, the mole I longed to kiss buried in the confusion on his forehead. I was happy to keep the connection going. I loved it when he touched me. I was blushing again, allowing myself to daydream. Not that I had spent my entire time at the base pining for the Sergeant. I'd had one partner after we'd first arrived. It wasn't love or anything, but we did enjoy a physical relationship for nearly a year. His name was Mike, and he'd been killed in an accident that had claimed the lives of four men on the base. I was starting to get a complex. Every man I became involved with seemed to find an early end. I'd kept to myself since then.

I looked up again to study the Sergeant's face. He was looking down at me with an intensity that kind of scared me, but got my heart pumping fast again, like when I'd heard him call out to me. It was as though he were working something out in his head, something he was desperate to tell me. He licked his lips.

"What is it, Jeff?" We were hidden from view, tucked into a tight corner positioned between two buildings.

"I need to tell you something, Sara." His voice trembled slightly.

"You're scaring me, Jeff. What's wrong? Is something wrong?" I placed both hands on his shoulders, I felt his whole body quiver.

A tear escaped the corner of his right eye. My bottom lip trembled. This was it. This was the moment. The electricity between us was indescribable. My mouth parted, my lips felt full, tingling in anticipation. His eyes shut hard releasing a river of tears as his face bent down to meet mine. Every part of me tingled now, my heart was in my throat, my breath mixing with his as our mouths inched closer and closer. His lips were softer than I could have imagined, his kiss deep and probing. I gave myself over to him, our lips sealing our fate. A warmth overcame me that I hadn't experienced since that first night with Joel many years earlier.

He pulled away after what seemed like ages. My lips felt hot, my body weak. I'd never fainted before, but was sure what came next qualified. My knees absolutely gave out, my eyes fluttered closed, the book fell from my hand and I collapsed at the Sergeant's feet.

Chapter Fifty-One

I awoke in my bed. Jeffrey was sitting at the edge, watching me. I smiled and touched his lips with my fingers. He smiled back.

"I'm sorry," he said. "I shouldn't have."

"No," I begged. "Please, don't say you're sorry." I knew if he meant it this was over. That all I would have experienced of our unspoken love would be that one and only kiss.

"Sara, I'm married. I have children." His face was the picture of despair. Was he unhappy with his life?

"Are you happy?" I asked.

"Right now I am happier than I've been in years," he admitted as he took my hand in his. "Sara, I've loved you for so long."

"I know. I mean, I've felt the same way."

"What do we do about it?"

Reality hit me. He *was* married. He *did* have kids. This was a small community. This sort of thing didn't happen here. "I don't know." I wanted to tell him I *did* know. That he should leave his lovely wife and family and be with me. But how?

"I shouldn't have," he began again and I heard a mournful groan that originated deep in his chest. His body shook to a convulsive, silent weeping. I sat up and threw my arms around him, squeezing him into me. I cried with him.

"We can make this work," I decided. "We can do this." I pulled his face back with both hands, unable to bear the thought of never kissing him again.

He kissed me then, harder than before, pushing me back onto the bed. He broke the kiss after too short a time and stared into my eyes. I didn't let him speak again. I drew my face up to his and kissed him in desperate successive breaths. My mouth veered from his mouth as I kissed his cheeks, his nose, the beautiful mole on his forehead, his neck. I was feral with emotion. Almost unconsciously I removed his shirt and unbuckled his pants. His boots fell to the floor with a satisfying thud as I realized he too was undressing himself.

Then his hands were on me, pulling at my shirt, pushing down my pants. I kicked off my shoes and arched my back in a race to be naked against him. His hot muscled flesh pressed up against mine and began to move rhythmically. My legs wrapped around his, my hips moving with him.

We made love for hours, until just before Leif arrived back from school.

I turned to look at Jeff. His eyes sparkled to life and he smiled. "I know," he said. "It's late, I should go."

"What are we going to do?" I smiled back at him sadly.

"Let me worry about that." I liked that he took charge, but this wasn't all on him.

"I don't want to be without you," I started. "But I can't let you leave your family for me." My head rolled to stare at the grey brick wall.

"This has been coming for some time, Sara. This isn't going to be a big surprise to her."

"I can't be the reason you leave your wife." I didn't know which would hurt more; living with the guilt of being a home-wrecker or living without Jeffrey.

"This isn't your choice alone, Sara." He raised himself on one elbow and looked down at me. "I *love* you. I'm *in* love with you and I can't hide it any more."

How I'd longed for this moment, for those words to come out of his mouth. Still, it was not perfect. Not while he was married to such a wonderful woman, a woman I respected.

"Don't do or say anything yet, Jeff. For me." I hated the words coming out of my mouth. I only meant to keep his wife from suffering this revelation tonight. I wanted to think of a way to not hurt anyone, but knew in my heart that was a silly dream. This would destroy his family and make us outcasts.

"I'll wait, but not forever. Not again, Sara." He kissed me gently, left the warmth of my bed, sweat glistening on his back. Once dressed he opened the door, looked down the hall and popped his head back in.

"I love you."

"I love you." My heart leapt as I spoke the words. With a cautious smile he winked and closed the door behind him.

I had only moments to lay in bed reliving the incredible event that had just occurred. Just as I was happily retracing his hands along my body, this body which had remained untouched for so long, Leif entered the room and began to undress for bed.

"Hi, Leif!" I caught him off guard.

"Mom!" He turned and threw his shirt at me. "Don't scare me like that!"

"Sorry, honey," I apologized. "I thought you realized I was back already."

"How would *I* know that?" He continued to change for bed, slipping a pajama top on next.

"Doesn't Blank Man tell you everything?" I kidded. Blank Man and I were a team now, with one direction: to instill a sense of destiny in my son.

"*You're* in a good mood."

"You think so?"

"You're practically *glowing*, Mom." That was as good an explanation as could be arrived at by an eight year-old boy.

"I guess so." I sat up gripping the covers tightly around my naked body. I patted my hand on the bed beckoning him over to sit. He walked over, and plopped himself down on the mattress. He touched my face with his little palms, tracing my features with his fingers. It was something he'd done since he was a toddler. When he came to my mouth I pretended to bite his fingers and he jumped back, smiling. We were both in a pretty silly mood.

"Mom, do you believe in love at first sight?" This was a timely question.

"Sure I do, Leif. Love can happen at any time, in any place. Are you in love?" His face scrunched up again and his tongue stuck out.

"No!" He continued to brush my hair with his fingers. "But someone told me they were in love with me."

"That's fun, honey. Who?"

"Sherri," he whispered, his head lowering as if he was ashamed to have told me. Sherri was his little friend from school. Sherri was the same girl who had lost her father in the terrorist raids.

"Sherri is a lovely girl, Leif. She is only six, a little young for you. But in ten or twelve years, that won't really make a difference."

"Mom! You're not helping! I don't *want* a girlfriend!"

"Okay." I laughed out loud. It was nice to see that the human condition hadn't changed so much. Boys and girls, whatever age, were still suffering the same drama as ever. "Just let her down easy though, okay?"

"But how do I do that? She's always grabbing at my hand in class and trying to kiss me." His little features crinkled up at the memory of her shameless advances.

"Leif, you just be *nice* about it. You tell her you're not ready for a commitment and that you would like some time to think about it. Trust me, this way she'll get bored waiting and pick another little boy to have a crush on."

"Okay, that might work. Thanks, Mom." He bounded off the bed and jumped up into his own.

"Sweet dreams, Leif." Sweet dreams. I couldn't remember the last time I'd had a sweet dream, but if ever I would again, it would be tonight. It had been so long since I had tasted true happiness, and tonight had left me longing for more. As much as I knew it was a torturous decision that lay ahead of us, all I wanted tonight was to sleep, feeling the warmth of Jeff surrounding me.

Chapter Fifty-Two

It had been two days since I'd heard from Jeff and I was becoming increasingly alarmed at the signals I was receiving. Every time our eyes met out in the openness of the parade grounds or in the crowded mess hall, he looked away. My heart fell sickeningly to the pit of my stomach each time. That he might have regretted our actions, gone back to his wife, told her he loved her and had decided to stay.

I had been on such a high the first day after our encounter. I had let him have his space while he decided on how to go about telling his wife, but had I pushed him away by not letting him break it off that same night? Did he think *I* didn't want to break up his unhappy home? I needed to talk to him, to tell him again that I loved him and convince him to do what was right for *him*. If that meant telling his wife everything and making a clean break to be with me then I had to believe that was the right thing to do. I deserved happiness too.

I was sipping coffee while sitting outside the hospital building between duties. Shielding my eyes against the sun, which had been burning up the clouds during the past week, I noticed Jeff strolling cautiously across the grounds towards me. I smiled automatically and thought I saw a smile on his face in return.

"Let's talk," he said abruptly, passing me on the bench and opening the door for me to enter.

My heart trembled and my stomach churned. My face sank as I passed through the open door and followed him down the familiar hallways and into the mess hall. He positioned us in an isolated corner. There were a handful of people milling about the hall. We didn't look out of place, but I felt very uncomfortable.

Standing across from him, I kept my head lowered. I found it difficult to look at him, hoping that if I didn't, I wouldn't read the bad news I feared he had come to give me. Then his hand was on my chin, lifting my head. I kept my eyes closed.

"Open your eyes, Sara. Please."

Tears escaped down my cheeks as I opened my eyes. His were hard, and all my fears were realized. My body shook uncontrollably and he took notice. I couldn't stop it. I was fighting the overwhelming urge to cry.

"Sara," he started, then paused. "Sara, please. You were right."

My teeth began to chatter, my chin quivering. The blood in my head pounded against my eyes, forcing more tears. Had I somehow convinced him to do the mindful thing and not follow his heart?

"Sara." He was reluctant to put his hands on me again for fear that the others in the hall might notice. I battled valiantly against crying out. My neck stiffened and a lump in my throat muted any attempt I might have made to speak. "Sara, please." He was embarrassed now by my inability to control my emotional response.

I wiped my face and sucked in a deep breath. I exhaled slowly and opened my stinging eyes. His expression oozed compassion.

"I love you," he whispered.

"But?" I managed, knowing full well something would follow.

"There's no 'but' about it, Sara. I *love* you." He paused. "And I love my wife." That was just as good as a 'but' to me. Where would I fit into that equation?

"You were right; she deserves more of an answer for my behavior. So do you." He leaned back and pushed his fingers through his short dark hair. "I'm confused."

"I'm in love," I said defiantly. "I'm in *love* with you, Jeff."

"And I'm in love with you, Sara."

"But," I said again, swallowing hard.

"Okay, listen, this is impossibly difficult for me, Sara. Yes, 'but'. But I love my wife. I went home after we – after, and there she was with the kids watching a movie and I realized I was not so unhappy. Not so much to ruin a whole family for my own selfish happiness."

"What about my happiness?"

"We can still be happy, Sara."

My brows met in the middle, confusion bubbling from within.

"I won't be a mistress." I blurted. I didn't want to sneak around, stealing a kiss or making love in secret. I would never get over the guilt of it. If he made a clean break, everyone could heal.

"What? No, I don't want that either. I want a solution. But I couldn't, can't do that."

"You *did* that already," I hissed.

"Yes, and I'm ashamed of it."

That was not what I wanted to hear.

"Then I guess we have nothing left to talk about." I couldn't imagine a more hurtful thing to say. With what little dignity I could muster, I left the mess hall, Jeff seated in the wooden chair. I didn't look back. I had been derailed from what truly mattered. My son, and his development into something great. That was my purpose here. I would never let my own petty desires for happiness intrude on that again.

Chapter Fifty-Three

The following week I made every effort to avoid the Sergeant while he made every attempt to find me. I found endlessly new and inventive ways of eluding his advances. I threw myself into teaching Leif the lessons I'd learned during my time with the old women in the bunker. It was all at once beneficial to both him and my state of mind. I spoke to the Blank Man, taking encouragement and information from him and relaying it to my son.

Spending so much time with Leif made me happy again. He had always been a source of happiness in my life. I'd look at him and I'd smile. It was just that simple. It was difficult to be depressed with a child who depended on your mood for their own comfort.

We visited the greenhouse twice a day and I let him sit with the Chaplain for hours at a time. He learned something new about the natural world every day and shared it with me over dinner. He also found comfort in the Chaplain's spiritual knowledge, pressing for more, asking questions and challenging him on his faith. The Chaplain was happy to engage Leif, and found their conversations very gratifying. One day in the greenhouse he confided in me that their conversations were as helpful for him as they were for Leif.

"It helps me understand my own faith when I can discuss it with someone as bright and curious as Leif," the Chaplain explained to me. "He is an extraordinary boy, Sara. He has questions that go far beyond his years."

"Leif has an old soul," was all I could reply. I wasn't sure if a man of God, based in Christianity, would ascribe to the idea of reincarnation.

"An *old* soul," he repeated. "That's an interesting concept. Not exactly what I preach. One soul, one life, one chance. That's the God I know."

"Is it limiting for you?" I asked.

"Was it for you when you *believed?*"

"I guess not. At least, not after the bombs fell."

"When did you lose your faith, Sara?"

"I don't like to say I lost my faith. It just evolved along with my experiences."

"It changed to suit your needs?"

I smiled up at him, his dark features thoughtfully smiling back at me.

"You know, I almost want to tell you a big secret," I nodded. "To get your take on it."

His eyes brightened. "But?"

"Well, the secret's really not mine to tell." My eyes fell to the cement floor which was slowly being overtaken by a crawling vine of some design.

"I won't press you, Sara. If you feel I could benefit you by telling me, you will."

"You're Catholic, so if I told you, you couldn't tell anyone else?"

"That's right. My confessional is absolute." He stopped and turned to face me. I stopped too to meet his gaze. "Sara, if you want to come see me tonight, I will sit with you and listen. If you'd like me to comment I will and if not, I will remain silent."

"I'll consider it." It would be nice to have an accomplice in Leif's on-going education. The Chaplain placed a hand on my shoulder and grinned widely.

"You let me know. It doesn't have to be tonight. I'm not going anywhere."

"Thanks." We walked towards where Leif and another boy were watching the fish dart back and forth in the raised pond as they flicked the waters' surface with their little fingers.

*****

That night, at dinner Leif questioned me about my conversation with the Chaplain.

"What were you talking about, Mom?"

"Oh, just the same kind of stuff the two of you discuss." I stacked our trays together and placed them on the neighboring table. I looked around and I could see Jeff and his family behind us. My face hardened as I turned back to my son. It had been excruciating being trapped in such close proximity to the man who had broken my heart, his wife, and his children. I had even thought about leaving. My primary concern was of course Leif and he was the only thing that kept me here. But every day I saw Jeff, the thought again reentered my head. Leif could apparently tell from the crease in my brow that I was preoccupied.

"Do you want to tell Chaplain about Blank Man?"

Jesus, was he reading minds now? I leaned into him and lowered my voice.

"What would you think of that, Leif? Would you want him to know?"

"I think he already knows actually." He finished the last of his granola bar and threw the packaging onto the trays.

"He knows? You told him?"

"No, I didn't tell him. But I have a feeling he knows. It's like he can sometimes see him, 'cause sometimes Blank Man sits with us when we're talking and gives me questions to ask."

"What makes you think the Chaplain can see Blank Man?"

"Sometimes he goes like this." Leif squished up his face, his nose shrinking as his cheeks rose and eyes squinted. "And looks in Blank Man's direction."

That was interesting.

"But Blank Man says not to tell."

I looked up turning in my seat.

"He's not here, Mom. He's just saying it in my head."

"Okay, honey. We'll follow Blank Man's instructions then."

"You *like* him now, huh?" A mischievous smile crept across his rosy cheeks. His head nodded as though answering his own question.

"Oh, yeah, we're like this now," I said with a smile, my fingers crossing. Leif smiled brightly and a giggle escaped his lips. I in turn snorted and we both started laughing. It was the kind of laughter that escalates the more you look at one another. People in the mess hall turned and looked, but this only made us laugh harder. Jeff was watching but I didn't care.

The muscles in my face ached after laughing so hard. I hadn't laughed like that in a very long time. I knew I had been wearing a frown almost every moment I wasn't with Leif. But right now I felt alive, and I would relish that moment in days to come.

*****

With the passing of another week I felt a little lighter. Time was healing my broken heart. I knew I couldn't feel this way forever. I had managed through my first love's death and this would be no different.

Leif was progressing brilliantly, becoming obsessed with meditation, taking a half hour three times a day to sit cross-legged, straight backed quietly humming to himself. How an eight-year-old had the patience for something most adults didn't have the patience to do I'd never know. I chalked it up to Leif being something special, something more. Just like the witches had prophesied. Like Blank Man had told me. Leif was going to be great.

It was in this state I found him one evening in our bunk room, seated on his bed, humming, eyes closed. But this time he did not break the meditation after his half hour was up. Nor did he break it at the hour mark. At two hours I became concerned.

"Leif," I said quietly from my bed, looking up from behind my book. "Leif, it's time to go to sleep, honey."

Nothing.

"Leif I need you to stop your meditation and go to sleep now." I put the book down and stood. "Sweetie, it's time for bed."

He did not acknowledge me at all. I gently placed a hand on his shoulder but was forced to snap it back. The electrical shock that I received was heart stopping. Amazingly, Leif did not budge. I positioned a hand above his head, afraid to touch him again. As my palm approached his crown, the hair on his head all stood on end.

"Leif," I continued, worried by this bizarre reaction. "You need to snap out of it, honey, please." I sat next to him and looked at his face. His expression exuded an absolute calm, the low rumble of his humming was hypnotic. I was careful not to touch him again but ached to hold him.

The humming got louder. Within a few seconds it was so loud I had to cover my ears. I got up and stepped outside the open door into the hall. I was scared to death at what was transpiring. There was no one in the hall to help me. I turned back to my son from the door way, his face glowing, radiating, and suddenly, as quickly as it had escalated, the humming slowed and with it the volume. I cautiously stepped back into the dimly lit room. Suddenly his eyes opened, the pupils tiny, as though he'd been in a very bright place far too long. I rushed to his side but stopped short of hugging him. I reached out a hand and it hovered. Something was pushing me back. We were like two magnets repelling each other. I could not get any closer to Leif. My palms felt hot and I pulled away. "What's happening!" I gasped, falling to my knees.

"Don't be afraid, Mommy." Thank God, his voice! "Don't be afraid." I stared at his face and realized the voice came from within him as his lips were not moving.

"Leif?"

His head turned slowly in my direction. His eyes found mine. Somehow I knew he was okay.

"What's happening to you, Leif?"

"Enlightenment."

Michael E. Poeltl

REVELATION – BOOK THREE of The Judas Syndrome Trilogy

Leif Speaks....

I watch an army camp among the trunks of dead trees to the west from my vantage point at the edge of this rocky hill, which was carved from an ancient landscape when the ice fields receded some twelve thousand years ago. The ruined forest offers modest privacy and even less protection should we decide to attack them before they do us. But the Sergeant and I have agreed that we are better suited to defend our position within the walls of our compound, rather than risk openly attacking a group so large and desperate.

My Blank Man is with me now. Blank Man is the name I gave to him when he first appeared to me at the age of six. I can feel his presence. Each time he appears the hairs on the back of my neck and forearms prick up. He is dark, and has no features save what I can make out of his silhouette. His voice is calm and soothing. Mom calls him my Guardian Angel, and he even has a halo of sorts. Not confined to his head, but surrounding his entire being. If I'd given him a face he would have one. But I have not in my twelve years of knowing him.

*****

Some months before I will be faced with the vision of an army at our doors, I find myself staring at the forests within our walls. They contain trees taller than our tallest building: pine, deciduous, fruit bearing, with birds and insects buzzing around. From the dust of my mother's Apocalypse, twenty years later, we have trees planted firmly in the soil. We have reestablished life where it was once devastated by a desperate, deliberate act of violence.

I have led a privileged life in comparison to those outside our fortified walls. To have grown up at all is a gift in the wasteland beyond our oasis. I have learned that life is a gift, and should be cherished, lived and experienced. Though experience often reveals itself as pain in this world, it is still purposeful, it still has its place in the evolution of our spirit.

*****

My name is Leif. I've been told that my father was meant for this end. But my father faltered in his attempt, afraid of this destiny, afraid of himself. It has been made clear to me that I was born to carry the torch - that the spirit of my father lives on in me. Though that phrase may seem cliché, it should be taken literally rather than figuratively. I am the reincarnation of my father. My angel has told me as much. And my mom has confirmed it, pointing out the bizarre birthmark on my right arm. It is a dark line that travels the circumference of the forearm, just below the elbow. Mom says this resembles a wound my father suffered not long before he died.

Additional Resources:

www.the-judas-syndrome.com- official website for the series

More books by Michael Poeltl

The Judas Syndrome (Book one)
Revelation (Book three of The Judas Syndrome)
Her Past's Present
Available on Amazon

About the author

Website: www.mikepoeltl.com
Twitter: @mpoeltlauthor
Facebook: Michael.Poeltl.author
Amazon Author Page: Michael Poeltl Amazon

Acknowledgements

Rose Keefe – Editor - www.rosekeefe.com
Thanks once more to my editor and friend, Rose, as she continues to assist me in my journey.